"So you think we can come to mutually acceptable terms?" Steven asked.

Tessa nodded vigorously. "I do. That's why I came rushing over. As vague as your mother can be at times, she seemed certain that you'd be more than willing to see me."

Steven whirled, regarding her with a sagging jaw. "My mother? You discussed all this in advance with my mother?"

"I thought you knew. Millicent handpicked me personally, it seems. I tried to speak to her, but she only talks in circles, doesn't she? So it seemed smartest to work things out with you."

Steven marveled at Millicent's nerve. "My mother can be pushy, and I don't always care for it, but this time she's done me a huge favor." He moved in closer, resting his hands on the arms of the chair so their faces were almost touching. "As a matter of fact, I'd like to tie you up right now if you're willing."

Tessa's small body stiffened in the huge chair. "Tie me up?"

"Believe me, this is how it's generally done, Tessa, at least in America. I can't go to sleep tonight on a maybe."

"You expect a bit on the side, on top of all the rest?" She gasped in dismay.

Weddings by De Wilde™

1. SHATTERED VOWS   Jasmine Cresswell
2. THE RELUCTANT BRIDE   Janis Flores
3. DRESSED TO THRILL   Kate Hoffmann
4. WILDE HEART   Daphne Clair
5. A BRIDE FOR DADDY   Leandra Logan
6. TO LOVE A THIEF   Margaret St. George
7. A STRANGER'S BABY   Judith Arnold
8. TERMS OF SURRENDER   Kate Hoffmann
9. FAMILY SECRETS   Margaret St. George
10. WILDE MAN   Daphne Clair
11. ROMANCING THE STONES   Janis Flores
12. I DO, AGAIN   Jasmine Cresswell

Weddings by DeWilde™

PREVIOUSLY AT DEWILDES

DeWildes in Sydney—The Store and the People...

- A new branch of the DeWildes chain in Sydney, Australia, is hardly a surprise. But a new branch of the family is certainly a shocking discovery!

- Natasha Pallas has accomplished her goal, and managed to return one of the missing DeWilde jewels to the collection.

- Along the way, she's managed to fall in love with Ryder Blake, the power and energy behind DeWildes' Australian venture.

Nick Santos, priceless bracelet in hand, is heading back to London, and another startling DeWilde secret!

Mary Schulz is acknowledged as the author of this work.

ISBN 0-373-82541-2

A BRIDE FOR DADDY

Copyright © 1996 by Harlequin Books S.A.

This edition published by arrangement with Harlequin Books S.A.

® and TM are trademarks of the publisher. Trademarks indicated with
® are registered in the United States Patent and Trademark Office, the
Canadian Trade Marks Office and in other countries.

Printed in U.S.A.

A
Bride for Daddy
LEANDRA LOGAN

Harlequin Books

TORONTO • NEW YORK • LONDON
AMSTERDAM • PARIS • SYDNEY • HAMBURG
STOCKHOLM • ATHENS • TOKYO • MILAN
MADRID • WARSAW • BUDAPEST • AUCKLAND

Dear Gabe,

Just a note to let you know that I'll be arriving from Paris next Wednesday, eager to begin my new entry-level position at the London store. Under ordinary circumstances I would expect a brass band and chauffeur to greet me at the airport. But I do still hope to prove my designer talents without family interference, so I'll gladly manage on my own. Give my best to all the relatives and ask them, for the time being, to please deny my very existence!

Your loving cousin,

Tessa

CHAPTER ONE

"I CAN'T BELIEVE YOU'VE settled in this Battersea flat when you could have your pick of all of London." Gabriel DeWilde appeared shell-shocked as he peeled off his mist-covered trench coat inside the doorway. "Tessa, this is the height of eccentricity, even for you!"

Tessa Montiefiori regarded her cousin with tolerant affection as she took his coat and hung it on a peg beside the door. She'd been postponing this tour of her place for nearly two months, knowing her modest life-style was going to be a tough sell to Gabe. But this particular Sunday night had apparently been the limit for him. He'd called to say he was coming by and had hung up before she could argue. "Oh, Gabe, how I wish I had a pound for every time you've called me eccentric over the years!"

"But this charade of yours borders on lunacy," he insisted, trailing after her into the small sitting area. "Masquerading as a struggling designer named Jones when you're part of the family. You could slip into a senior position at DeWilde's tomorrow if you liked. As merchandising manager for the store, it would be my pleasure to arrange it."

"So you said six weeks ago, when this all began. But my feelings haven't changed. If I can sell my wedding designs to the finicky critics and the public without revealing that I'm family, it will prove my talents are genuine. It will also help stop the wagging tongues of store employees who'd undoubtedly complain that I got ahead because of nepotism. It's my most inventive challenge yet, don't you think?''

"Yes," he relented on a sigh. Tessa had been on the loose for three years since university, first working at entry-level positions in some of America's West Coast fashion houses, then landing in Paris to apprentice with a top designer. Gabe had visited her in both places, all the while holding on to the hope that she'd come home to work with him. Well, she'd finally done so, but on her own terms. "To tell you the truth, Tess, when you first announced you were coming home, I had hoped you were ready to take your place at DeWilde's—as a member of the family, I might add—and had gotten over your experimental phase.''

"It's not a phase!" she exclaimed, affronted. "I intend to test myself with new challenges and new situations over and over again my whole life through. It keeps a person fresh."

"The idea of collecting modest pay packets each week and living in this glorified boarding house seems unnecessarily inconvenient." Gabe cringed at his surroundings. The plaster walls were cracked, the wooden floor was worn, and the fireside chairs flanking the sofa no doubt dated back to the Battle of Mons.

"This is the perfect setting for a shopgirl," she said, countering his inspection with stubborn approval. "And besides, I *like* it. I couldn't be more settled, here or at DeWilde's. So why are you making a fuss now, right before my contest is about to begin?''

He looked hesitant. "It's the contest I'm thinking of. There's still time to announce who you really are, before the press comes in tomorrow to cover the Experimental Boutique's wedding package giveaway."

"This is the moment I've been working up to, Gabe, the chance to model my dream wedding dress and show off my talents."

"Think of the embarrassment you'll face if someone recognizes you as a Montiefiori before you're ready to come clean."

Tessa shrugged. "I don't expect to get caught. I haven't lived in London for years—since before attending boarding school in Switzerland. And I was a different person then, with fifteen pounds of baby fat and my hair cropped to my ears. That tomboy image is long gone."

Gabe couldn't argue the point. Tessa's svelte figure and lush, strawberry blond mane were the epitome of femininity.

"The charade should be over in a matter of days," she said, giving him an encouraging pat on the back. "The publicity from the contest should bring in quick reviews of my talents. Once I know where I stand, I'll reveal my true identity. Okay?"

"Even if the news is bad?"

Optimistic by nature, Tessa hadn't envisioned losing. "Yes, I suppose so. If I fall on my face, I'll just have to reevaluate my situation. Maybe transfer to the New York store and pose as a Smith," she suggested jokingly.

"Right." He gave her long French braid a tug, and wandered over to the second-story bay window overlooking White's Row.

With a confident air, Tessa folded her arms across her chest. He'd find nothing to complain about out there. Even in the gathering dusk, it was obvious that the whole street was in tip-top condition, with tidy lawns and gardens fronting the restored nineteenth-century houses.

"Who owns this place, Tess?"

"A charming old widow named Mrs. Mortimer. She converted it into four flats several years back for financial reasons—and for the company, I think. I absolutely adore her," she confided excitedly. "She embraces her tenants like cherished relatives."

He half turned, revealing his handsome profile. "Just what you need," he teased. "More relatives."

Admittedly, there were plenty of those between the Montiefioris and the DeWildes. But Tessa's mother had died in an airplane crash when she was just a toddler, and Mrs. Mortimer satisfied a hunger inside Tessa for maternal attention.

"I wish you could just be happy I'm back, Gabe— support my plan, even if you don't completely approve of it."

He faced her with a full smile. "You can count on me. And I didn't come here simply to complain, either. I want to see the wedding gown that you've been keeping under wraps."

"I thought you'd never ask!" She walked over to her work area near the bay and moved a three-paneled Japanese screen away from her dressmaker's dummy. The headless form was wearing her dream creation, a stunning white dress with an off-the-shoulder lace bodice and a full, frothy skirt of crepe de chine.

Gabe's eyes gleamed with approval. Tessa's passion for life and her willingness to take risks brought a freshness to her work. "Fabulous job—very innovative. It's exactly the sort of thing the store needs more of."

Tessa grew more animated as she showed off the garment. "See these tiny pleats at the waistline? Don't they give the skirt the illusion of multiple layers? And what do you think of this delicate cross-stitch at the shoulder?"

"You're a master of detail. This premier design will give you a name, I know it." He paused as he passed her small kitchen nook. "Say, is that stew I smell?"

Tessa wrinkled her upturned nose, testing the air. "Yes, it is."

"Don't tell me you've taken up cooking!" Ignoring Tessa's sound of protest, he wandered into the kitchen nook, peering into the pots on the stove. "There's nothing in here!"

"Of course not. It's Mrs. Mortimer's stew. Her flat is directly below, you see."

He reappeared in the doorway between the two rooms. "It's as if she were cooking right here in your flat."

"This is a rambling old house. Sounds and smells travel throughout."

"Well, in any case, it smells wonderful. She must be a pretty good cook," he relented, striving to be positive.

"Oh, she is—and very generous. One call downstairs and she'd be dashing up with a brimming kettle. We have a bartering arrangement, you see. I hem her skirts, clean the stairwells, things like that. In return she feeds me on occasion." She snapped her fingers with inspiration. "Tell you what, if you agree to be Gabe Jones, poor cousin to shopgirl Tessa Jones, I'll call down for dinner."

"Lianne's expecting me at home."

"We'll give her a call, too. She can be Mrs. Jones to your Mr."

Gabe's forehead furrowed. "You are and always will be the most irritating female on earth!"

"It's always been my pleasure to torment you," she said sweetly. "It's been rough having to behave in the store and keep a cool distance from you. It's the only chink in my whole plan."

Gabe watched Tessa circle her creation, checking lengths with the whisk of a tape measure, removing stray pins with practiced efficiency. He couldn't help but think how beautiful and graceful she was, and that she should be tormenting a suitor rather than her cousin. It seemed incredible that some man hadn't fallen hard for her yet. But he also realized that it would take a special man to come up to Tessa's standards. She approached life head-on, demanding and passionate, and her quest for the unconventional could be intimidating to most men. As much as Gabe knew she cared for him, and as close as they were, he could feel her pulling further out of his sphere of influence with every passing year. Tessa was unquestionably her own woman.

Undoubtedly, it would take a hell of a strong man to initiate a romance. Of course, it would be different if she spotted someone she wanted. The poor blighter wouldn't have a chance! Gabe stroked his chin, tilting his head back a fraction. The more he thought about Tessa in love, the more he warmed to the idea. Tessa needed a husband, a solid, dependable man who could take the fluttery edge off her wings and ground her slightly. Of course, he'd been so blissfully happy since his marriage to Lianne the previous summer and only wished that everyone else in the world could be half so fortunate....

"A penny for your thoughts, Gabriel."

Gabe was startled to find her regarding him suspiciously, snapping her tape measure taut like a piece of rope. "I was merely thinking that you're bound to need me less and less with every passing year," he replied.

"Oh, poor darling. As it happens, I can use your help right now." She beckoned him closer. "Mind the hemline, now."

Gabe closed in on the billowing garment with the greatest care. "Want me to carry this dummy someplace?"

"No, I want you to press the tip of my tape measure right about here." She guided his hand to the dress's waistline, where the pleated crepe de chine was sewn into the lacy bodice.

She would only want the tip of his thumb! He reluctantly dropped to his knee beside her, thinking of the dozens of employees who could assist her once she took on a senior position. "I hope this whole farce is worth it."

"Most of the work is done. Everything for my contest and the wedding package giveaway is in place for tomorrow's launch."

"*Your* contest? You're still calling it that, are you?"

She frowned at his odd look. "What's that supposed to mean?"

"I thought you knew. Shirley Briggs has taken credit for the entire promotion—"

"She what!"

"Oh, it's common practice down in the Boutique. Shirley uses her managerial position to glean ideas from all the fledgling designers like you. She stood before me with a straight face several weeks ago, outlining your plan to spotlight a new designer with a store-sponsored contest. She said you were chosen for the promotion because you'd be such an attractive model and had a suitable dress in the making."

"I was chosen because the whole thing was my idea!"

"I didn't know that for sure at the time," he said defensively. "You hadn't said a word to me, so I didn't dare call her a liar."

Tessa squeezed her eyes shut as her temper boiled. "That's what I get for doing the right thing, trying to go through the proper channels. How can she get away with this over and over again?"

"I assume it's because the designers don't want to risk losing their apprenticeships. Unfortunately, I can't take action without proof. It's a serious charge. I don't know how that woman ever came to be working for us in the first place. She's a total misfit—completely contrary to all DeWilde's stands for—and as soon as we have legitimate grounds for her dismissal, she'll be gone. Until then . . ."

Tessa threw her arms up in despair. "Oh, Gabe, this is awful!"

"You know, what that department needs is someone with the right personality and marketing savvy to turn it into something super, something that would take DeWilde's into the twenty-first century."

Tessa's green eyes took on a knowing twinkle. "You're appealing to my ambitious streak, Gabe, and you're not being very subtle about it."

"So, take me up on it. Give the press some real news tomorrow."

She shook her head firmly. "No, I want that impartial appraisal first."

"All right." He straightened up again with a sigh. "You seem to know what you're doing. The dress is certainly lovely." He slipped his hand into the pocket of his tweed jacket with an inscrutable look. "It's a shame to have so much bare skin on display with this plunging neckline, however."

"You're beginning to sound like an old married man protecting his own!"

"Hmm, I wouldn't mind bundling up Lianne to hide her from prying male eyes," he admitted candidly. "But that's not what I meant."

"You're playing at something," she realized. "What is it?"

"I was just wondering how this bauble would look nestled above your décolletage." He withdrew a blue leather jewelry box from his pocket and opened it. Nestled in the velvet lining was an antique pearl choker. It was exquisitely designed, with a huge, perfectly symmetrical pearl in the center and alternating strands of smaller pearls and diamonds.

Tessa gasped in pleasure. Her father, George Montiefiori, had handed down some of the family heirlooms to her and her three siblings, and she'd received this particular necklace. After university, when she began to travel, she had given it to Gabe for safekeeping. "How thoughtful of you to bring it along!" Gingerly she took the pearls in hand and rushed to a round, brass-framed mirror hanging on the stark plaster wall.

Gabe's reflection joined hers as she attempted to secure the clasp. "Let me help." He fastened the necklace with ease, accustomed as he was to handling the family jewelry. "You wear it every bit as well as Celeste must have."

She adjusted the choker over the crescent-shaped birthmark in the hollow of her throat, a mark that she shared with the grandmother, who had all but abandoned her father and grandfather long ago. Tessa could not imagine making such a choice herself, though she'd inherited Celeste's independent streak. "It is just the accessory for my wedding dress. My promotional dress," she hastened to clarify as Gabe smiled approvingly.

"That's just what I was thinking. You can tell people that it's DeWilde property and we lent it to you for the week."

"Yes, all right."

His brows arched in hope. "Perhaps you'll wear it for your own wedding one day."

"Oh, Gabe!" She huffed in loving disgust. "Ever since you and Lianne tied the knot, you can't see anyone being happily single."

"Guilty as charged." Pleasure flushed his features.

"Well, I'm perfectly content on my own," she stated firmly. "I absolutely adore waking up each morning without the slightest idea where the day ahead will take me."

"Loving Lianne has only made my life better. Somehow, some way, I'd like to see you settled with someone worthy of you."

Tessa whirled around and stood on tiptoe to press a finger against his lips. "Chase those thoughts straight out of your head. Matrimony is the furthest thing from my mind right now. I'm a career woman through and through!"

CHAPTER TWO

"OH, LOOK, GRANDMA MILLY," young Natalie Sanders squealed excitedly. "Over there!"

Millicent Sanders rose from the walnut bench where she'd been resting just inside the entrance to DeWilde's and glanced in the direction that her granddaughter was pointing. Beyond the cosmetics counter, shoppers were milling around a model dressed in a bridal gown and standing atop a rotating pedestal.

Natalie sighed dreamily. "She's got to be a princess."

Nicky nudged his sister with his elbow. "A Cinderella mommy."

Millicent was not surprised by their fanciful conclusions. Fans of fairy tales, they considered England to be the far-off land where their favorite characters lived happily ever after. Understandably, this world-renowned wedding store, with its elegant decor and polished display cases of glittering jewels, would represent an enchanted kingdom in their innocent minds. Add one pretty model dressed in an elaborate, off-the-shoulder wedding gown, her blond hair wound into a burnished crown beneath a pearl headdress, and you had the personification of a fairy-tale heroine.

And the sort of dream mother the pair so desperately longed for.

The children began to pull on Millicent's thin wrists, anxious to join the action. "But we only stepped in here so I could sit down and catch my breath."

The children groaned. "Oh, Grandma. Please!"

"All right." Millicent followed in good humor, despite her weariness. In her turquoise Chanel suit, her silver hair cut in a fashionable wedge, she appeared far younger than her seventy years. Unfortunately, she felt every bit her age, and was finding it increasingly difficult to keep up with the children's nonstop pace. But for the moment, she was the only mother figure they had, and would do justice to the role until her widowed son Steven had the good sense to remarry.

Naturally, being in a store that specialized in weddings only heightened Millicent's longing for a new daughter-in-law. How glorious it would be to guide the bride-to-be through DeWilde's imposing entrance, beyond the hallowed blue doors, across the glossy marble floor. Credit card in hand, Millicent would be ready to pick up the tab for the very best DeWilde's had to offer.

"What's happening?" Nicky demanded, jumping up and down for a better view as they joined the crowd gathered around the model.

A stout middle-aged woman dressed in a gray cloth coat turned to address them. "DeWilde's is sponsoring a wedding ensemble giveaway."

"You talk different," Natalie observed, her delicate face alive with interest. "Just like the man driving that funny black taxi. He steered us all around on the wrong side of the road!''

"This is their first trip abroad,'' Millicent explained apologetically. ''They're visiting from New York City. On a business trip with their father.''

The Englishwoman's broad face glowed with understanding as she surveyed the excited youngsters. Fragile, spindly limbed Natalie looked the height of femininity in a pink dress, lacy white ankle socks and black patent leather shoes, her long brown hair adorned with a ribbon. Sturdy little Nicky was an all-American boy in a rust pullover and dark slacks, his blond hair clipped short and his face round and dimpled. Despite the two-year age difference between them, Nicky was already catching up to his six-year-old sister in height and weight.

The woman crouched down beside them with a pleasant expression. "Where's your mum, then?''

"She's in heaven,'' Natalie replied just above a whisper, clamping her slender hands over her younger brother's ears. "It's hard for Nicky to understand about Mommy,'' she added, giving her puzzled brother a kiss on the cheek before he managed to wiggle free.

Millicent noted the woman's distress and touched the sleeve of her coat. "It's all right to speak of my late daughter-in-law, really. Renee's been gone for three years.''

The woman brightened, once again at ease.

"Can we get closer, Grandma?'' Natalie pleaded.

Holding their hands tightly, Millicent edged her way through the people circling the display.

Nicky's jaw dropped in wonderment. "Is she for real?''

Natalie shrugged. "She's gotta be somebody important. But who? Cinderella? Snow White? Alice? Do you know her, Grandma?"

"I just might...." Millicent's reply faded away as she studied the petite model and extravagant pearl choker with interest. Both seemed familiar to her from another place and time.

"C'mon, Nicky," Natalie urged, grasping his small square hand in her slender one.

Lost in her own thoughts, Millicent distractedly cautioned them to be polite as they advanced to the velvet cordon surrounding the pedestal. Damn these tired old eyes of hers! For years she had enjoyed perfect vision. She clicked open her boxy handbag and extracted her wire-rimmed bifocals. Raising them to her face with a fluttery motion, she perused the young woman through the nearsighted glass, then the farsighted glass, paying special attention to the pearl choker at her ivory throat.

Sure enough, the model bore an unmistakable resemblance to her old friend Celeste Montiefiori, who also happened to be a descendant of the DeWilde family. The two women shared the same upturned nose and well-defined cheekbones. And weren't those the pearls that Celeste wore regularly with her more revealing dresses to conceal the birthmark in the hollow of her throat? Why, Millicent had worn them a couple of times herself, to the Cannes film festival in the seventies and to Ronald Reagan's inaugural ball in the eighties. They had shared so many good times! But as with all her old friends, contact with Celeste was infrequent these days. Millicent's family duties kept her stationed in New York City, leaving her little time for extended travel or social chitchat.

How intriguing to see the necklace again. Millicent didn't believe for a single minute that Celeste would entrust it to anyone but her own flesh and blood. Millicent was the only person with whom she'd ever shared the choker, and only then because Millicent had been so insistent.

Perhaps the model was a grandchild, daughter to Celeste's son, George. He had three girls and a boy, if memory served her right. And DeWilde's was a family operation, with various members of the family working in the store's five branches.

Millicent had first met Celeste more than twenty years ago in the south of France. Celeste was recuperating from a broken love affair with an Italian film director and treating herself to the best with his farewell payoff.

Unlike Millicent, who was rooted in family ties first, last and always, Celeste had proved to be more or less detached from her relations and saw herself as unable to cope with any real responsibility. She spent her time and energy indulging in risky liaisons and a lavish life-style, courtesy of the extravagant gifts and goodwill she managed to glean along the way.

To their mutual surprise, the two women had taken an instant liking to each other. Despite their different circumstances, they'd become fast friends, rendezvousing for chatty lunches and social events in the years to come.

Millicent considered those days some of her best, when she and Robert were well connected socially. Their toy company, Sanders Novelties, had been an American mainstay specializing in family board games since the late forties. Founded by her father-in-law, Gerald, the business had been handed down to

Robert, ultimately landing in the hands of Steven. As much as she adored caring for Steven and his brood, being abroad and thinking of Celeste made her heart yearn a little for what had once been.

"May I help you, madam?" A plump, middle-aged woman in a gold taffeta shirtwaist had paused before Millicent. Her features were sparrowlike, and she had a beaky nose and dark beady eyes; her sleek brown hair was swept up in a chignon.

"Do you clerk in this department?" Millicent asked graciously.

The woman beamed with pride. "I am Shirley Briggs, manager of DeWilde's Experimental Boutique. Shopping for a wedding, are you?"

"I hope to be in the near future," Millicent hedged. "For a relative." A workaholic son who didn't know any better.

Shirley shifted the wicker basket she was carrying from one arm to the other, the pink brochures bearing the DeWilde name sliding around inside it. "You've come at an opportune time, then. We are currently featuring a storybook wedding giveaway."

Natalie appealed to the older woman with unmistakable longing. "Is she a real fairy princess?"

Shirley Briggs found the idea highly amusing, her bosom shaking with suppressed laughter. "Certainly not. She is a young apprentice designer here in the boutique, modeling one of her own designs. The dress itself is the center of the giveaway, you see," she explained to Millicent. "We are attempting to draw customer and media attention to our up-and-coming in-house talent. The winner of the contest will receive a gown identical to that one and everything else to make a dream wedding come true, from reception to honeymoon.''

Nicky turned round, his blue eyes squinting with suspicion. ''Bet she lives in a castle.''

Shirley's patience was thinning with her smile. ''Not likely. She is a shopgirl of modest means.''

''Then she probably is Cinderella,'' Natalie told Nicky in congratulation. ''She was poor at first, you see. Then the prince came along and gave her her shoe back and they had a real big wedding.''

Nicky leaned over the rope and tipped his blond head up in an effort to peek at her feet beneath the frothy hem of the dress. ''I can't see her feet, Natty.''

Natalie turned back to Shirley Briggs. ''Will you ask her to lift her dress, please, just a little bit?''

Shirley inhaled sharply. ''She is acting as a human mannequin and doesn't move or speak to anyone!'' Then, not wishing to appear too short-tempered, she turned back to gush at Millicent, ''Such imaginations.''

But Millicent wasn't listening. The model had moved a bit, craning her neck slightly, just enough to reveal a familiar birthmark on her throat. Throwing vanity to the wind, Millicent set her glasses firmly on the bridge of her nose for a better view. Sure enough, the small brown crescent was identical to Celeste's and in a similar position near her collarbone. This was more than enough to verify Millicent's suspicions. She had to be a Montiefiori!

But why in heaven's name was this clerk in the dark about it? Shirley Briggs referred to her as a shopgirl. The mystery behind this masquerade was intriguing enough to pursue a little bit. ''What is her name?''

"Tessa Jones," Shirley supplied, taken aback by what seemed like an inconsequential question.

Tessa... If memory served her correctly, Celeste had three granddaughters, Vanessa, Catherine and... Tessa! That was it! "Forgive my curiosity, but is Jones her married name?"

"She is still single. Most of my young designers are married to their work at this stage."

Natalie's smile broadened as she locked eyes with her brother. "Wonder if she likes children."

Nicky's smile grew. "Yeah..."

Millicent knew full well that they thought the bride herself was part of the prize. If only it were true! Celeste had always insisted that her granddaughters were indescribably sweet-natured. And this girl obviously had talent and ambition. Steven could do a lot worse, stumbling through the social scene on his own. Who was she kidding? He had done a lot worse. Over and over again with deliberateness.

How she'd love to steer him Tessa's way with direct honesty, bring him to the store, introduce them. But he'd long since tired of her matchmaking attempts. If he were simply living in a lonely limbo, hoping that the right girl would come along, she'd accept it. But he was proving hell-bent on clubbing the nights away with no direction. He claimed that it was all harmless fun. But Millicent felt it was only a matter of time before a female predator grabbed hold of him and spoiled everything. Taking Steven out of circulation again, putting him in the hands of a woman as worthy as his late wife, Renee, had evolved into her most important mission in life.

Natalie sidled close to Millicent wearing a determined look on her face that Millicent often saw in

Steven when he had a bright idea. "Grandma, I think this might be a good deal for us."

Millicent touched her granddaughter's long brown hair. "I agree." They turned their full attention to Shirley, whose face was alive with curiosity. When Millicent offered no explanation of their circumstances, Shirley began to outline the contest rules.

"It's a case of writing down, in one hundred words or less, why you think you deserve DeWilde's storybook wedding package. It is my understanding that our merchandising manager, Gabriel DeWilde, will judge the entries and make the final decision."

"We love our storybooks," Nicky squeaked with shining eyes.

"It's a real-life story we're after," the literal clerk clarified, reaching into her basket for a brochure and handing it over to Millicent. "There, you see," she said as the older woman opened the pink paper. "A place for your composition."

Millicent read the fine print through her bifocals. "I fill this out and return it to you, then?"

"Exactly."

"Any tips to offer?" Millicent asked, with just a dash of helplessness.

Shirley openly enjoyed being consulted. "I would advise a catchy title for starts, something the public will easily identify with. The management would like to reward a worthy recipient, of course. Having a dramatic story to tell will no doubt help." She leaned closer. "DeWilde's wants to have an impact on somebody, change the course of someone's life."

Millicent and Natalie exchanged a smug little smile. Drama was a Sanders specialty.

"I'm afraid you'll have to hurry," Shirley went on. "The deadline is five o'clock this afternoon. The drawing is scheduled for tomorrow afternoon at noon, you see, and all the essays must be sorted through. I hope you don't feel it's too late."

Millicent's smile deepened. "On the contrary, Ms. Briggs. Being an optimist, I figure I'm just in time!"

Shirley Briggs moved on and Natalie collected a reluctant Nicky from the velvet rope.

Millicent fingered the brochure, pursing her lips. She should tell the children the bride was not included right here and now. But it would probably discourage them from entering and spoil any chance of bringing Steven and Tessa into the same orbit. Besides, they all needed an adventure. Especially Steven. He'd been working way too hard lately in a quest to find a European distributor for his Galaxy Ranger action figures.

"What are we going to do now, Grandma?" Nicky asked.

"Have a little lunch and decide how best to tell our story. You can start thinking of a catchy title on the way to the restaurant."

Natalie paused with a faraway look. "'A Bride for Daddy.' How does that sound?"

Millicent gasped in approval. "How clever, Natalie!"

Natalie glowed with pride. "This isn't going to be hard at all."

"The hardest part will be keeping it a surprise. I insist you don't tell your father."

"Surprise?" Natalie groaned in protest, folding her arms across her chest. "We like to tell Daddy everything."

"I know you do," Millicent agreed with a slight groan. Every nip of sherry, every subway ride, every feast of fatty ice cream was promptly reported to their frazzled father. "But we don't want to get his hopes up until we've won. There will be plenty of time for celebrating if it all works out."

STEVEN SANDERS RETURNED to his suite at the London Hilton Hotel on Park Lane about four o'clock that Thursday afternoon. No sooner had he removed his key from the lock than Natalie and Nicky came charging out of their bedroom and across the sitting room.

"Daddy!" they chorused, wrapping their small arms around his middle.

"So, how was your first day in jolly old England?" he asked, his bright blue eyes crinkling with pleasure as he kissed their heads with sound smacks.

"Really good!" Natalie chirped, her small face shining. In keeping with their Fifth Avenue apartment ritual, she handed her father's briefcase to Nicky and began to tug at the sleeve of Steven's gray cashmere suit jacket, easing it off his broad shoulders with a rustle. "How was your first day in jolly old England?"

"Just fine." Steven allowed the children to guide him across the rich cream carpeting to a pale blue settee. They sank to the cushions together, Steven's lap considered fair game to the squirmy pair. As they nuzzled one another, he noted that they were already wearing their pajamas. "Isn't it a little early for the pj's?" He glanced over at his mother, who was seated across the room at the cherrywood writing desk, and noted that she too was wearing her purple satin loungewear.

Millicent shrugged, barely glancing up from the *Times* crossword puzzle set before her. "They wore them for their nap and it seemed unnecessary to get dressed again."

"I planned to take all of you out to dinner tonight."

Millicent released a dramatic breath, as though just crossing the finish line of a marathon. "They are completely exhausted."

Steven grimaced over the lie. It wasn't the first time in recent weeks that Millicent had pulled this stunt because she herself needed some rest. If only she'd accept her own limitations! But she refused to, now more than ever. She was playing the all-star mother figure to the hilt so he wouldn't make good his promise to hire a live-in nanny. But he was determined to find a suitable one during this London trip and bring her home on the plane next week, if possible.

"We have a big surprise, Daddy," Nicky announced brightly. "Real big."

Steven gazed at Nicky's chunky, guileless face and then at Natalie's slender, coy one. "Tell me all about it."

"It wouldn't be a surprise anymore if we did," Natalie exclaimed, indignant.

Millicent stiffened in her straight-backed chair. "Can't argue with the girl's logic, Steven."

"I suppose not," he relented, tweaking Natalie's nose. "So, how long will I have to wait for the bombshell—I mean, the pleasant but unexpected announcement?"

"Nothing to concern yourself with," Millicent assured him breezily. "Just child's play, really. How was the meeting today?"

"Fine for starters, I guess." Steven stretched and groaned, leaning his head back. The moment he did so, he could feel his son's small hands raking through his freshly clipped hair. The children made a game of searching for gray strands among the brown. The count was on the rise. "I think Butler Toys is interested in my proposal," he speculated. "It's still too soon to be sure of anything. Franklin Butler's British reserve makes him tough to read. But at least the ball's rolling. I brought in some sample Rangers—"

"You got some dollies in here?" Natalie had already dropped to her knees and transferred the briefcase from the coffee table to the floor for easy access. She pushed back the twin gold catches with her thumbs and lifted the lid.

"C'mon now, Nat," Steven protested. "The Galaxy Rangers are action figures."

Natalie pulled two twelve-inch action figures dressed in space cadet uniforms off their bed of file folders. "I only play with dolls."

"I like monsters," Nicky growled, grabbing the male figure from his sister.

Steven chuckled. The children continually managed to humble him with their artless observations. Their reactions to his cherished creations would astound the employees at Sanders Novelties back in New York, who saw him as a miracle worker for pulling his father's company out of bankruptcy and saving their jobs. The line of superheroes had major sales back in the United States and was now saturating the market with syndicated cartoons, comic books and traveling ice shows.

"What's so funny, Daddy?" Nicky asked. "I'm tryin' to scare you. Rrrr..."

Steven's chuckle deepened. "You're probably the only boy on earth who makes Captain Lance Starbuck growl like a werewolf!"

"A visionary just like his father," Millicent suggested proudly.

Nicky raised the figure's arms and launched an attack on Natalie, known to be easier prey. "Hairy monster's gonna get you!"

"Stop it!" Natalie cried indignantly, leaping into her father's lap. "Make him stop, Daddy. It's not funny! He's a behavior problem."

Steven pried the children apart, settling them on either side of him. "When I agreed to get you out of school for this trip, you both agreed to behave. Remember?"

"Kindergarten is a much bigger deal than preschool, Nicky," Natalie boasted, leaning over her father. "In kindergarten nobody makes the boy dolls act like monsters."

Nicky retaliated with another "Rrrr..."

"I try to teach him!" Natalie cried out dramatically. "Boy oh boy, do you need a real mommy. Boy oh boy—"

"So, Steven," Millicent interrupted anxiously. "You were saying about the business meeting? Is this Butler Toys outfit the one to manufacture and distribute the Galaxy Rangers over here?"

Steven stretched his legs out on the coffee table before him. The children followed suit, imitating him down to his deep-rooted groan. "Their merchandising team seems set to go. The only glitch is the conservative board of directors and owner Franklin Butler. After months of faxes and phone calls, he's still not sure of the product's potential in the European market.''

Millicent was shocked. ''Why ever not?''

Steven lifted his hands in a helpless gesture. ''He hasn't given me a straight answer yet.''

''But surely your decision to come here and make your pitch personally should expedite matters.''

''Mother, not everyone perceives me as the silver-tongued charmer that you do.''

''Fiddlesticks.'' With a wave of her pen, Millicent returned to her crossword, squinting at the clues.

Steven regarded her with keen interest. There was something unusual about her behavior tonight that he couldn't quite pinpoint. Was she hiding something behind that puckered forehead or merely struggling with seven across?

As if sensing his suspicion, she squinted all the more. ''Steven, give me a four-letter word for malt liquor froth.''

''Mmm . . . Barm.''

''Yes, perfect.'' She made a show of filling in the blanks, then set the pen aside with a clack. ''There, that's done.''

''Did you really finish it?'' he asked in delight.

''I filled in all the blanks. I guess that's the goal.''

Steven was visibly impressed. ''What a wonderful new pastime for you, Mother.''

She released a noncommittal sigh. ''Not necessarily. I was just feeling a little fidgety tonight and thought I'd give it a try.''

"The papers at home have wonderful puzzles. There are books devoted to them, too."

"So?"

The frostiness in Millicent's tone was meant to chill him to the bone. It was her most severe way of cautioning him. She'd be furious to know that the technique had lost its impact by his twelfth birthday. "I didn't mean anything. I simply thought you might be in the market for new activities."

"I'm busy enough, thank you."

But they both knew all that was about to change. With a nanny in place, she'd be freed up almost completely. On the loose and more desperate than ever to find him a suitable wife. A shiver raced down Steven's spine at the thought of the bevy of debutantes bound to be on his doorstep.

"I just thought that if you excelled at crosswords—"

"To be honest, not everything connects the way it should." Millicent rose from her chair, the bell sleeves of her purple pajamas billowing like wings as she stretched her arms over her head. "I went wrong someplace and couldn't make it all fit."

"Using a pencil would help a lot. That way you could erase mistakes and balance things until they do click."

"I'll give it all the consideration it deserves," she promised with a cleverness that didn't elude her son.

"But—"

"I'll order up some dinner," Millicent suggested, gliding toward the bedroom she shared with the children.

"Order spaghetti," he called after her with a wink to the children. "Enough for all of us."

"We get to stay up?" Natalie asked hopefully.

"You bet." Steven ruffled his daughter's hair, his smile playful. "I thought we could exchange surprises."

"You first," Nicky said with a pat to his father's knee.

"Okay. Franklin Butler gave me a new card game he has on the market. It's a bigger version of your old maid game, with some extra rules. It's in my case, under the folders."

Natalie found the deck and spread the colorful, oversized cards out on the coffee table. "What's a real old maid?"

Steven smelled a trap but answered her, anyway. "It's an old-fashioned word for a woman living alone. You know, like in the game. The old maid doesn't have a match in the end."

Natalie's mouth puckered sadly. "Just like you, Daddy. Grandma says you don't have a match. You're all alone in the end, too."

Steven's smile grew strained. "Old maid is a term for unmarried ladies only."

"They call you an old man, then?" she persisted.

"No, Natty! I'm just a man—and your proud father." This line of thinking was all his mother's fault. If only she'd stop referring to their family unit as incomplete. Steven was capable of supplying the children with all the love and support they needed. They'd proved to be flexible and appeared well adjusted. If only he could sell his current life-style to his mother. Make her see that losing one wife in a lifetime was all he could handle.

"We'll have to play this game," Natalie enthused, peeking at the cards.

"Sure, right after we eat." Steven leaned closer to his daughter, who was seated at his feet. "Now," he said softly, "do you have a surprise for me?"

"Well . . ." the girl said slowly, her pert nose wrinkling. "We promised not to tell."

Steven tensed. He wanted to know what was up, but dreaded it, too. With his mother in place as the madcap mastermind, it was bound to mean trouble for him. "C'mon now, spill. What happened today?"

Millicent strolled back into the room, magically on cue. "I took them to a few of the larger stores—Harrods, Harvey Nichols. We also dashed into Asprey for a gold bracelet. A very ordinary day."

Nicky made a noise of protest. "Don't forget the princess bride. Did you forget her, Grandma?"

"Certainly not." Millicent fluffed her gray hair and sent a significant look to her son. "I could hardly forget a fairy-tale princess."

A tale. Steven exhaled with equal measures of relief and irritation. Millicent was signaling him that the surprise was of the make-believe sort. She'd most likely been trying to keep it a secret because he'd disapprove. "Now, Nick," he began, attempting to reason man-to-man with his son, "how many times have we discussed the difference between those tales and real life?"

"I'll show you, Daddy." Nicky scrambled off toward the bedroom he shared with his sister.

He returned within seconds, carrying the family's worn copy of *Cinderella,* along with his threadbare security blanket. He bounced back into his father's lap and began to leaf through the dog-eared pages. In an excited babble he drew his father's attention to the color sketch of their heroine making her entrance at the ball.

Steven's forehead furrowed. "I don't understand."

Millicent cleared her throat. "I was feeling a bit tired walking the streets, so I took the children into DeWilde's to sit for a few minutes."

Natalie beamed with pride. "I saw her first. Cinderella standing on a shiny throne. In a beautiful white dress, all fluffy and shimmery."

"A human mannequin," Millicent translated. "Naturally, the children wanted to see her up close. Naturally it sparked their imaginations."

"Would you like to see her, Daddy?" Natalie wondered.

Steven loosened his tie, aware that all eyes were fastened on him. The only sound was Nicky's sniffle as he rubbed the frayed corner of his blanket under his nose. "I don't think I'll have time."

"Would you let us keep her, Daddy? If we got her fair and square?" Natalie's fingers formed a steeple beneath her chin.

Steven blinked in amazement. "I doubt she's for the taking!"

"Yes or no, Daddy," Natalie persisted. "Yes or no."

"I'm sure she's just a store employee doing her job—"

"But what if she's not? What if she's a real princess looking for a home?"

It all seemed so silly, but it obviously meant the world to them. "Okay, you can keep her. But," he went on above their squeals, "if that falls through, I want you to treat your new nanny like royalty." The trio groaned, Millicent the loudest. He addressed his mother with resolve. "I spoke to that Bond Street agency today about setting up some appointments for tomorrow afternoon. The woman assured me that their employees are fully trained and very pleasant."

Millicent waved him off in disgust. "A Sanders has never resorted to hiring child-rearing help."

"It's a necessity, pure and simple, Mother. The subject is closed."

"Did you at least check on Mary Poppins, Daddy?" Natalie asked.

Steven rubbed a hand over his weary face. "No, baby, I didn't."

"We told you to!" she cried in disappointment. "She'd be almost as good as the princess mommy."

Steven slanted his mother a dark and dangerous look. Mary Poppins was one thing. The princess was another. But the mention of a mommy really lit his fuse. What the hell did she think she was doing?

"Natalie, darling, Mary Poppins is out the question," Millicent asserted, hoping to calm her steaming son.

"But why? She seems just right. And she's practically perfect, you know." She reached over and patted Nicky's arm. "You'd like to feed the birds with her, wouldn't you?"

Steven cupped Natalie's chin in his huge hand. "Mary Poppins doesn't really exist."

Natalie's voice climbed with her temper. "We saw the movie and read the book. She lives in London! Everybody knows that! Why won't you just call her up?"

Steven rubbed his hands over his face. "She has an unlisted number."

Natalie pried his fingers open for a glimpse of his expression. "You aren't crying under there, are you?"

CHAPTER THREE

"SORRY I'M LATE—" Tessa paused in midsentence at the doorway of her cousin Gabriel's sixth-floor office that evening as she spied a splash of gold taffeta near the window. Shirley Briggs was here! When Tessa exchanged her wedding dress for a worn rose sweater and leggings, she'd assumed this meeting to sort the contest entries would be a family affair. She hoped her airy greeting and casual clothing hadn't blown her cover and aroused Shirley's suspicions.

Gabe, dressed in a gray business suit, was seated behind his huge, ornate desk, which was all but buried beneath a heap of pink brochures. Judging by the twinkle in his eye, it was clear that he was enjoying Tessa's discomfort. "Right. So nice of you to join us, Miss Jones."

"Yes, good evening, Tessa," Lianne chimed in on a note of sympathy.

"Hello, Lianne." Tessa smiled at Gabe's wife, who was seated in a leather chair opposite her husband's desk. Lianne looked absolutely radiant in the red A-line dress that Tessa had designed and sewn for her months earlier. The crimson jersey drew out the reddish sheen in Lianne's chestnut hair and complemented her pinkened complexion. But Tessa couldn't tell her how wonderful she looked in her creation, for Shirley would never understand why one of her employees would make Gabriel DeWilde's wife such an expensive garment in the first place. Instead, she talked shop. "The headdress you designed for my gown was a smashing success. I heard lots of compliments from my rotating perch."

"I'm thrilled to hear it. As it happens, we're just deciding on the winning essay," Lianne reported. "Being the pivotal force behind the promotion, we thought you'd like to be present."

Be present? Despite Shirley Briggs's presence at the window, Tessa sent her cousin Gabe a condemning look. He knew she wanted to be in on the selection process. She'd read each and every entry before sending them up here and had firm ideas on who should be the winner.

"Miss Briggs," Gabe said in a bid for her attention. "Shall we give Tessa the good news?"

"Of—of course." Shirley Briggs turned then, a brochure in one hand and a man's handkerchief—presumably from Gabe's empty jacket pocket—in the other. "I am so sorry," she blubbered. "But I am so overcome by this particular entry that I—" She broke off to trumpet into the snowy fabric, the initials GDW now apparent on the bottom corner.

Tessa took great delight in watching Gabe cringe over the beating his handkerchief was taking, as did the good-humored Lianne, who covertly sent Tessa a wink. And seeing iron-pants Shirley in this emotional state was nothing short of amazing. The peevish manager was crumbling before their eyes like a dry macaroon!

"I apologize, sir, but the poor mites... wanting a new mum decked out right and proper." Shirley once again gave her beaky nose a mighty, manly blow. "If

I had children and they lost me, it would be so difficult for them.''

Tessa stepped up to take the brochure from Shirley's trembling hand. Her surprising interest in children was obviously more theoretical than workaday.
Tessa couldn't begin to count the times the manager
had treated them with cool indifference on the floor.

'' 'A Bride for Daddy?' '' Tessa perused the creative and emotional plea written in a childlike scrawl.

> Please help us! Our daddy needs to marry a
> princess. Our real mommy is in heaven and he is
> very lonely. He is also very busy and doesn't have
> time to make up a whole wedding. We promise
> to live happily ever after. Thank you.

Tessa released a breath, lifting her eyes from the page.
"I admit that it's a clever approach. But do we want
this sort of gimmickry?"

"Now, Tessa," Lianne reasoned, "these children
sound very sincere and are bound to be charming. So
far we're all in complete agreement they should win."

Gabe nodded enthusiastically. "I was instantly
moved by the childish penmanship and the simple
message. Nothing else even came close."

Tessa's face was nearly as flaming as the tide of
reddish-blond hair framing it. Since when were these
two so mushy over strange children? Had the whole
DeWilde side of the family gone mad? First her Uncle Jeffrey and Aunt Grace had separated, and now
their characteristically unsentimental son was melt-
ing over the plight of a single daddy he'd never met!

"I was thinking along other lines entirely," she
dared to object with a petulant set of her chin.

"There's a Chelsea girl whose fiancé is stationed overseas. It's her dream to have a wedding all set for his next leave."

"Another worthy cause, certainly," Lianne agreed.

"And she is the kind of single working girl the Experimental Boutique is trying to attract—"

"Your opinion has been noted, Miss Jones." Gabe cut her off with a firm reminder of how little her opinion counted under her self-imposed anonymity. "The rest of us have taken a liking to this family about to acquire a new wife and mother. And don't forget that we're looking for good advertising copy. A real tearjerker that the media can pick up and expound on, a romance to warm the coldest heart."

This was news to Tessa, who was merely looking for a spotlight for her design. She immediately sprang from her chair. "How much time will I be expected to spend with the winners—these children?" she demanded.

"Exposure to the little ones will be minimal, surely," Lianne consoled. "A few shots of the family. Fielding questions from the press. They'll probably be clinging to their father's bride-to-be."

"All you'll have to do is stand around in the dress for a few more hours looking lovely," Gabe added.

Shirley preened at Gabe as she spoke to Tessa. "Mr. DeWilde has promised to make this essay contest a biannual event if all goes well tomorrow. Isn't that generous of him? The least you can do is follow his directions to the letter."

Aware that Tessa had reached her limits of endurance, Gabe pushed back his chair and rose. "I have every faith that you'll handle the winners with the kind of flair and dignity worthy of DeWilde's."

Tessa shook the hand he extended, wishing all the while that she could toss him judo fashion right over his fancy desk.

"IT SEEMS OUR LUNCH has arrived." Franklin Butler's voice boomed through his own boardroom the following afternoon as a delivery man entered with a box of sandwiches.

Steven smiled to himself. Barry Lambert, his closest associate at Butler Toys, had clued him in on Franklin Butler's habits. Lunch was delivered to his office every day promptly at twelve-thirty. If the long, polished conference table wasn't cleared for the meal, he all but swept it clear with a beefy arm. Knowing how important personal touches could be in business, Steven had deliberately timed his presentation with care, so it would not conflict with the designated lunch time. He'd spent most of the morning outlining the many spin-off products his action figures were currently generating, producing samples for inspection. He had ended his speech fifteen minutes ago, giving the six executives present a chance to examine everything.

Now, as the directors put their notes aside for their midday meal, he paved the way for his afternoon sales-figure presentation. As prearranged, Barry began to collect the various Galaxy Ranger posters, comic books and lunch boxes, returning them to Steven's boxy display case. In the meantime, Steven unzipped his portfolio and withdrew a large tablet of colorful graphs, which he placed beside his chair until lunch was over. His gaze strayed for a moment to the heavyset Franklin Butler, who held the fate of the deal in his hands. Butler looked a bit like a satisfied walrus with his slicked gray hair, white sideburns and flabby jowls. He was all smiles now as he passed out the wrapped sandwiches and offered tea and coffee. If only Steven could step into Franklin's mind for sixty seconds and find out what his reservations about the Galaxy Rangers were.

"Mr. Sanders?" Judith, the company reception-ist, had sidled up beside him without making a sound, the model of warmth and efficiency in her sensible wool dress and cap of neat black curls. "Sorry to disturb you, sir, but your mother is on the tele-phone."

Steven's brows shot up. How could Millicent stoop to pestering him today of all days, when he was mak-ing the big push—and especially after the confronta-tion they'd had late last night?

Judith looked apologetic. "She did ask if you were on lunch break, and I said yes."

"Problem, Steve?" Barry Lambert joined them at the head of the table.

"My mother is on the line."

"I hope I did the right thing," the receptionist said. "She sounded . . . rather excited."

That had to spell trouble. "Thanks, Judith, I'll speak to her."

"Very well." She retrieved the gray console tele-phone from the bookshelf beneath the window and positioned it beside him on the table. Three lights blinked at once. "Yours is line two." With a bolster-ing smile, she eased out of the room, whisking the door closed.

Barry pushed back his dark suit jacket to hook his thumbs in his striped suspenders and regarded Steven with sympathetic amusement. "I suppose she's calling to see if we're up to more mischief."

Barry had been the source of last night's bitter argument with Millicent. The children were long asleep when Barry showed up at their hotel suite shortly after eleven to pick Steven up. Intent on keeping tabs on his social moves, Millicent had deliberately dozed on the settee, dashing to the door to admit his English pal. A few well-placed questions and Millicent had deftly tagged Barry—horror of horrors—a fun-loving bachelor. Close to Steven's age of thirty-seven, he'd had years to root himself deeply into London's party scene.

The men would have probably gotten out unscathed if Barry's two female companions hadn't come up from the lobby just then to hurry them along. They proved to be especially earthy in their language and referred to Millicent as the "old thing." This had led to a private row between mother and son. Millicent simply could not understand why a single father would waste time dating anyone who wasn't a potential mother for his children. Round and round they went on the old familiar track.

He hadn't spoken to her since. She and the children had been sound asleep when he left the suite with all his equipment, dressed in his best double-breasted charcoal suit. He hadn't expected to hear from her, either. She could hold a grudge with amazing staying power.

Steven reached down, punched the second button and snagged the receiver in a brisk, businesslike motion. "Hello, Mother."

"Thank heavens I caught you!"

"Is something wrong?"

"Of course not. And after last night, I think you owe me a pleasant word."

Steven smiled tightly at the businessmen seated round the table. They were just settling into their meal, and with nothing else going on, they were all focused intently on his phone call. But it could go deeper than that, he realized. They might figure that if he couldn't handle his own mother, he couldn't handle an expansion project, either.

"Why are you calling?" he inquired silkily.

"I was hoping you could spare your lunch hour. Spend it with us."

"We're having an in-office lunch today."

There was a pause on the line. "Oh, no. I hadn't counted on that."

"Where are you, Mother?"

"At DeWilde's—"

"DeWilde's again!" He reddened, realizing that the room had fallen completely silent at the mention of the bridal store. Not a cup or sandwich wrapper stirred. It never ceased to amaze him how curious people were about romance in general. He was in no mood to explain about his mother's matchmaking notions and his children's fairy-tale obsession. "What brings you there?" he pressed.

"The children wanted to show you the princess. It's the final day of her appearance—"

"It's not possible for me to come."

"I'm afraid I went too far. I told the children you'd probably be able to slip away."

His heart lurched as he heard a pair of familiar chirps in the background—Natalie telling him to hurry, Nicky calling out for him to bring Cinderella's shoe. "Mother? Mother, I wish you hadn't done that." Steven couldn't believe Millicent's nerve. She'd been pulling every control lever at her disposal lately, springing surprises, disseminating guilt. It was as though his decision to hire a nanny had caused her to short circuit. She saw all chances of getting another daughter-in-law slipping through her fingers and it angered her to the depths of her soul.

Unfortunately for her, Steven had reached his limit. "As much as I'd like to join you, I simply can't," he went on to say smoothly. "Please explain to the children. Have a nice lunch, and I'll see you this evening—" The dial tone sounded in his ear then, but he couldn't resist adding an "I love you, too," for appearances. Hoping he still resembled the capable businessman he was, he sank back into his chair, unwrapping the roast beef sandwich set before him.

"Are you keeping something from us, Sanders?" Franklin Butler inquired from the opposite end of the table.

Steven's pulse jumped. Here comes the probe from the chairman of the board himself. "What do you mean, Franklin?"

"I couldn't help overhearing that your mother's over at DeWilde's. Thought perhaps you have a wedding in the works."

"My family is always looking for adventure." Steven took a bite of the sandwich, finding he had a severe case of dry mouth, something that hit him at his tensest moments. If only he could get over the fear that the world was trying to marry him off against his will.

Judith had returned to circle the table with a full coffeepot. "I imagine there are lots of curiosity-seekers over at that store today. It's my understanding that they're sponsoring a contest this week, giving away a wedding, dress and all.''

"Almost makes one want to dash out and grab hold of the first available maiden to come along!" Barry quipped, earning a round of chuckles from the fatherly group, who were long since accustomed to his solo life-style.

Steven thanked Judith for the refill, pondering her information as he sipped from his office-issue mug. So there was a contest at the store. Then, the children hadn't been exaggerating the pomp surrounding the model bride they'd seen. She probably did resemble a princess. Steven felt his taut stomach muscles relax. There was nothing to worry about. Even if his mother had entered the contest, and—heaven forbid—managed to win, he didn't have a bride to take down the aisle. He was out of the woods on this one.

DEWILDE'S WAS HUMMING with excitement as Gabe gave Tessa a boost onto the pedestal for the last time. Lianne was acting as her faux maid of honor, arranging the lustrous silk skirt in a shimmery cloud at Tessa's feet, adjusting the headdress of her own design atop Tessa's crown of strawberry blond hair, double-checking her artistically made-up face.

"Good luck, Tess." Lianne squeezed her bare shoulder and stepped to the side to join Gabe. Tessa studied the couple with affection: Gabe in his jet black tuxedo, his light brown hair combed away from his strong features; Lianne in an emerald georgette shift that deepened the blue of her eyes. They were so excited. As was Shirley Briggs, who was handing out souvenir garters and mini bottles of bubble bath shaped like champagne bottles to the crowd.

Gabe switched on his portable microphone, calling for everyone's attention. "Welcome to De-Wilde's first wedding ensemble giveaway...."

Tessa's attention drifted as her cousin went on to explain that the purpose of the Experimental Boutique was to offer the consumer cutting-edge fashion at affordable prices. She scanned the crowd of customers gathered around her and couldn't help wondering who had written the winning essay. There were quite a few children on the floor today, making it difficult to even hazard a guess.

"And the winner is..." Gabe reached into the inside pocket of his jacket and extracted the familiar pink brochure. "'A Bride for Daddy.'"

The crowd erupted with noise. There were disappointed cries and hoots, which were swiftly overtaken by a stronger hum of anticipation. Tessa glanced over the sea of faces, homing in on the trio who most likely were the winners. A chic senior citizen in a gray Saint Laurent suit had hastily picked up the phone on the cosmetics counter and was already speaking to someone. She had two small children at her sides, a girl in a frilly blue dress and a younger boy in dark slacks and a bright red sweater. Both were meeting Tessa's stare with starry-eyed wonder. They couldn't have appeared more adoring if she were Father Christmas himself.

Gabe's smooth baritone came over the speaker system again. "A Bride for Daddy. Will the author please step forward."

Tessa watched the woman hang up the phone and bow her head to confer with the children. The young girl threw her hands up and began pushing her way through the tangle of people on her own.

A path cleared for her as she called out in a loud, clear voice, "We win! We win!" She reminded Tessa of herself at that age, her feet tapping on the marble floor, her shiny hair ribbon and ruffled hemline flying.

Gabe helped her up on the round pedestal and bowed to show her the essay. "You wrote this, then?"

"Oh, yes. My grandma helped me spell the words, and my brother Nicky helped me make them up." Natalie grew shy as she met his gaze, and her voice dropped to a whisper. "Do you really like it?"

Gabe's smile broadened. "Very much. Would you like to read it to everyone?"

"Will you help me?"

Gabe chuckled along with the crowd. "All right." A hush fell over the floor as everyone strained to hear her small voice, faint at times as she wavered from the microphone. When they finished, Gabe gave her a gentle push in Tessa's direction. She eased in beside the bride. Photographers moved into position, lining up shots.

Gabe handed Tessa the essay and she in turn presented it to Natalie. "Why don't you hold this up for the pictures."

"Whatever you say, Cinderella."

"Tessa, love. My name is Tessa."

Natalie smiled endearingly, thinking to dip in a small curtsy. "Yes, Your Highness. If you like that name better."

Tessa gulped nervously. "I'm not who you think."

Natalie turned her attention to the crowd, blithely ignoring Tessa's response. "C'mon, Nicky!"

Nicky, hard to miss in his bright sweater, became the focal point of the crowd's attention as he hesitated halfway up the path blazed by his big sister. Voices around him swelled in encouragement. Openly frightened, he remained frozen in place.

"Oh, c'mon now," Natalie crooned sweetly. "Just look at this dress. It feels just like your binky blanket." Tessa gasped as Natalie took a handful of crepe de chine and scrunched it in her fingers. "Soft and snuggly."

Gathering his courage, Nicky launched himself forward like a miniature missile, hopping up on the stand before Gabe could offer him a hand. Tessa caught hold of his shoulder, amazed at how solidly he was built.

"She says she's not Cinderella," Natalie cautioned him.

Nicky's eyes grew wide with realization. "She's gotta be."

"But I'm not, young fellow," Tessa assured him through her frozen smile for the photographers. Bulbs flashed from every angle, refueling her confidence. This was the moment she'd been waiting for. This would lead to the recognition she longed for.

Her triumph was shattered moments later, however, when Nicky unceremoniously hiked up her skirt to provide a revealing glimpse of her shapely legs. Before she could recover enough to readjust the crepe de chine bunched at her waist, another round of flash bulbs went off, capturing the moment for all time.

"You shouldn't have done that!" With a soft cry of dismay she whisked her skirt back in place.

His small features crumpled at the betrayal. "You already got two shoes."

"Of course I do!"

"My daddy is supposed to bring you a shoe," Nicky said with a forceful shake of his head. "So we can live happily ever after."

"What!" Tessa felt like a drowning woman, plunged into a sea of confusion. Questions from the media became more personal. When she directed a silent appeal to Gabe, all he did was lift his fingers to his mouth, urging her to keep up appearances. It was too late. No matter how she posed, it was bound to be the cheesecake shot that would be splashed across the papers.

When the reporters began to question the children in earnest, Millicent deftly moved in between them. "The children have nothing more to say," she announced, resembling an incensed Lauren Bacall in her pencil-slim suit. "Their father is my son Steven, and he will handle any details—"

Reporters on a feeding frenzy cut her off.

"You the gran, then?"

"Where is the father?"

"Your name Sanders, like the kiddies?"

"This ceremony is over," Tessa attempted to call out over the din.

Gabe took her cue and stepped up to make the broadcast over the address system. "Thank you all for coming. DeWilde's appreciates your interest and continued patronage."

Tessa, her headdress askew and the children enfolded in her skirt, tried to make her escape. "Nice to meet you, poppets," she said with a tug on her skirt. "Your father can come in anytime to discuss his prize." She edged closer to Gabe, who still held the microphone in his hand as he prepared to make his final remarks.

"We'll be sure to give you all the details about the fairy-tale wedding won by these two children for their lucky dad," Gabe concluded. "Until then—"

Natalie circled her arms around Tessa with a loving look and leaned in Gabe's direction. "And she is going to be our new Cinderella mommy."

The little girl's announcement boomed over the address system, causing pandemonium. Reporters and customers turned back to the little group huddled on the pedestal with renewed interest. What had been a heartwarming story was now worthy of a soap opera drama!

"Uh-huh." Nicky tilted his head up toward the mike, enjoying the sound of his own echoing voice. "We're engaged with her!"

CHAPTER FOUR

"PLEASE TRY AND understand, children. I'm not part of the prize." Tessa glanced at the gold watch on her slim wrist to see how long they'd been at it with the Sanders family. A whole twenty minutes into an emergency meeting in Gabe's office and matters still seemed hopelessly tangled.

Natalie stood by a low bookcase near the door, her lower lip jutting out a mile. "You gotta be! My daddy is the rich Prince Charming and he's coming to get you! Then we'll all live happily ever after in New York City."

"No, darling, no." Taking care with her frothy gown, Tessa crouched down to the girl's eye level. "You're just caught up in the dazzle of the moment. Surely your father is set to marry a love of his own. She will wear this dress and live happily ever after with you."

Natalie curled her hands into small fists, her face flushed pink. "You don't understand. You should try harder!"

Pity and frustration welled in Tessa. The child was quaking in her patent leather shoes, fueled with anger and on the verge of tears. She felt the very same way. Her contest was about to go down the tubes because of this mix-up! She twisted to gauge her cousin's state of mind. Gabe had been on a slow simmer since Natalie announced her father's impending engagement to her—or, rather, "Cinderella." That had been the turning point to real disaster. The peekaboo incident with the dress could have been laughed away, but the assertion that she—Tessa—was involved with the winner... It smelled of an in-store setup.

But hadn't she been the one who'd objected to choosing an essay written by a child? She had known it was risky, to say the least. For the first time ever, she'd been the voice of cool-headed wisdom!

Tessa wearily rose to her feet again, hoping to appeal to Millicent. "Mrs. Sanders, I am very anxious to contact your son."

"That's the spirit," Millicent agreed, lifting her teacup. "Later on would be best. When he's finished with his business. When you've had a chance to freshen up."

"Freshen up!" Tessa gasped in disbelief. "If we don't send out a press release immediately, naming his bride-to-be, the whole city will have us on our way down the aisle."

Millicent's eyes grew round above the rim of her china cup. "That slipup would certainly entangle the two of you, wouldn't it?"

"Without a doubt."

The old woman made an attempt at apologetic noises. "If only he could tolerate interruptions. But the overworked dear is in the middle of a huge deal. We're Sanders Novelties, you know."

Gabe angled an arm along Millicent's high-backed chair, leaning close to her ear. "I'm sure he'd be happy to hear from us this very minute. Why, we have the best of news to deliver. He's won the works!"

"Rest assured, no one needs the works more than my Steven."

Gabe straightened up grandly. "Well, then. Where is this meeting of his taking place?"

"Oh, I'd need his permission to tell you that." Millicent set her cup in her saucer with a clink, seemingly oblivious to their groans. "But there is one matter I'm personally prepared to clear up without delay." She smiled as their faces lit up. "I insist you call me Millicent. We're going to be seeing a lot more of one another, and there's no reason to stand on formality."

"That is very sweet," Tessa said with forced grace.

"Now, if you'll excuse me, I must visit the ladies' room."

Gabe appealed to his wife, who was sitting behind his desk, fingering Tessa's headdress. "Go with Millicent, will you, darling? We wouldn't want her losing her way."

Or speaking to any more reporters. Lianne could read his train of thought with ease. She stood, draping the headdress over his open appointment book. "Come along, Mrs.—Millicent."

Gabe ushered them out, closing the heavy door with a disgusted shove. Tessa joined him for a private word. "What's the old girl up to, Gabe?"

His eyes hardened. "Well, we really can't fault her for not wanting to interrupt her son if he's in the midst of an important business deal."

"But you don't believe her helpless act, do you?"

"Not for a second, Tess. For some reason she seems determined to interfere in her son's life—and has dragged our promotion into it."

"If only we knew what *his* plans were."

"Maybe he intends to elope and she wants to force him into a big wedding. Maybe he's avoided setting the date and she's giving him a shove."

"But why do the children insist I'm part of the deal?" Tessa demanded. "And why is Millicent endorsing the idea?"

"Perhaps they don't like the girlfriend," Gabe surmised. "Your participation could spoil the works, I suppose. No better time to find out, I'd say." Deciding to use the dowager's absence to his advantage, Gabe turned his attention to the children. The boy was hovering near the chair Lianne had vacated, gathering the nerve to touch the veil set out on the desk. The girl was stalking round with her thin little arms folded across her chest. "Now then, Natalie." He rubbed his hands together enthusiastically. "We're sure to hit it off, don't you think?"

Her forehead puckered. "Why?"

"Because I chose your entry. And, well...I'm sure to be a daddy myself one of these days."

Natalie's face brightened with hope. "What's your name again?"

"Mr. DeWilde, like the store. But you can call me Gabe, if you like. Now, surely your father already has a real-life girlfriend, doesn't he?"

"He has lots of girlfriends," Natalie said. "He is very, very popular."

"He must have a favorite," Tessa insisted. "Who did he go out with last?"

"Some lady who talks like you. She peeked into our bedroom last night and said, 'Oh, they're ever so big, and so much bother once they start talkin'.'"

Tessa frowned at Gabe. "She doesn't sound like fiancée material."

Natalie made a tsking sound. "Grandma never wants to see her again. I heard her say she'd sweep that bimbo right out of the door if Daddy saw her again."

Tessa heard a rustle of tulle and whirled around to find Nicky buried beneath her headdress. His eyes shone beneath the folds of sheer netting. "Do I look like Casper the Friendly Ghost?"

"Careful, lad, that veil's worth a fortune!"

"Don't yell at him!" Natalie cried out in alarm.

Tessa gasped, the child's reprimand startling her. "I'm not yelling."

"Don't you want us?" Nicky squeaked. "Why'd she change her mind, Natty? Did we do something bad?"

Natalie reached her limit then. Tears sprang to her eyes, quickly streaming down her cheeks. "All Nicky knows is that he needs a new mommy. He doesn't even remember our real mommy. Can't you see that?"

Panic-stricken, Gabe begged her, "Please don't cry."

Natalie gulped and shuddered as the tears poured down. "I'm not crying! I'm really strong, just like my daddy."

Overcome with compassion, Gabe picked up the featherweight girl and set her down on the sofa flanking the wall.

Tessa lifted the veil from Nicky and seated him next to his sister. "Now, then..." she began awkwardly. "Nicky, I don't think you're a bad boy at all. As for you, Natalie, love, it's plain to see that you're taking on far too much here and it's upset you."

Natalie's mouth sagged and her hands fluttered in the air. "I can't worry about me. I have my grandma and my baby brother to take care of all the time!"

Tessa shook her finger at the little girl. "If you want to help them, you have to tell us what's happening here. Is your essay the truth or not?"

Natalie hung her head. "Oh, yes. Daddy is too busy to make up a whole wedding. And our mommy really is in heaven."

"Does he know what you've done for him?" Gabe asked.

"No, Mr. Gabe, it's all a big surprise."

Tessa smiled hopefully. "But for it all to get started, there has to be some kind of wedding in the works, right?"

Natalie took the tissue Gabe offered and wiped her nose. "If you ask him nice, I'm sure he'll say yes."

"You can't have expected me to really marry him!"

"Why, sure," she said matter-of-factly. "What would we do with just a dress?"

"You have a point," Gabe conceded as Tessa looked forlornly down at her cherished garment.

Tessa turned to her cousin and spoke in hushed tones. "Gabriel, why would Millicent Sanders pick on me?"

"Who knows!"

"Well, I intend to get the truth out of her."

Gabe took hold of Tessa's arm, recognizing the familiar light dancing in her eyes. A showdown between the two strong-willed women was more than he could stand to watch. "Listen, it's senseless to go another round with the old girl at this point."

"Why? We've got the goods on her now."

His eyes narrowed to slits. "She's too diabolically clever for you. She's obviously prepared to handle any glitches in her plan with a lying turn of her tongue."

Tessa was openly insulted. "I can be a diabolical liar, too!"

"Don't I know it, shopgirl. But she's had more years of practice and has turned this into her show. If only we can reach the son before this goes any further—" Gabe broke off as Lianne returned with Millicent. His wife's distraught face alone spoke volumes.

"It's already hit the airwaves," Lianne announced. "The afternoon news is announcing the whirlwind proposal given Tessa at DeWilde's. 'A visiting Yankee businessman has wooed a young British designer with an essay written by his own children. He's won her heart, her dress and a wedding by DeWilde's.'"

Rocked with fresh anger, Gabe paced around the room. "It's sure to be in the evening papers. We'll be the laughingstock of the city!"

Natalie's ear-piercing scream bounced off the walls in stereo. "You're not nice at all! You're the bad guy!"

Gabe smarted under her accusing glare and extended finger. "I am not! I have responsibilities—to stockholders, bankers, relatives."

Tessa touched his jacket sleeve. "Now, Gabe, maybe I can fix things and somehow save the contest."

Gabe kept his profile to her, staring out at the slate gray rooftops as he struggled with his temper. "How?"

"I don't exactly know," she said reluctantly. "But it can't hurt to go ahead and track down this Steven Sanders for starters. He has a nerve letting his family loose in our city. At the very least, he should have to answer for it. Make good the damage done!"

"London Hilton on Park Lane," Millicent spoke up helpfully, her hearing apparently still in top form. "Room 807. After five is best." With an airy farewell, she rounded up the children and herded them out the door.

Gabe turned to watch her leave with open awe. "Damn, she's good."

"But what exactly is she playing at?"

"Who knows? Just remember that she's accustomed to winning."

Tessa tossed her head defiantly. "So am I, cousin. So am I."

"YOU WILL GIVE US A CALL, won't you, Mr. Sanders?"

Steven's reply was noncommittal as he all but whisked the fifth nanny applicant out the hotel door, almost closing it prematurely on her ballooning bottom. She was nearly as old as his mother, spoke with an annoying chortle, and believed in hearty fiber meals and lemon juice laxatives to "keep the pipes clear." Hardly his idea of a sweet but sensible caregiver.

He wandered back into the room with a glance at his watch. Five-twenty. He'd spent the past three hours conducting interviews and had come up empty. With a beleaguered sigh, he sat on the edge of the writing desk and toyed with the red tie slashed across his crisp white shirt. What rotten luck. Each and every applicant had seemed wrong for one reason or another. The first one had been too masculine, the next too flighty, the next too rigid. And oh, that fourth one, he thought with a knowing nod, she'd been hiding something! What this country needed was its own version of "America's Most Wanted." The show rounded up fugitives like cattle back in the States!

His confident nod dissolved to an ambiguous shake. Perhaps he was going about this all wrong. Any of the first three candidates would probably have been fine. Yet he wasn't satisfied. He kept seeing them through his children's eyes and sensed they'd be disappointed. But what was a widower to do, short of remarrying? Magically come up with a solution? Not likely, considering that his belief in magic had died three years ago along with Renee. So what was left?

A sharp rap on the door drew him out of his reverie. One last applicant? The agency had been unsure of the exact number, promising close to a half dozen. Maybe this one would be the charm. He eased to his feet, pinched the crease in his dress slacks and took several quick strides to the door, whisking it open.

"Steven Sanders?"

"Yes." Steven's eyes widened as he took in the small slender blond in the violet trench coat.

"I'm ... Tessa Jones." She announced her name tentatively, gauging his reaction. Amazingly, he didn't make any instant moves, like closing his hands around her throat or pulling her inside by the hair. Obviously he hadn't seen the evening papers.

He actually seemed more intrigued than angry.

Intrigued and intriguing. He was lean and fit, towering over her by a good twelve inches. His hair was cut a little short for her taste, but it flattered his sharp, even features. And though her weakness was for brown eyes, she had to admit there was a vividness to his blue ones that made her knees knock.

Steven cleared his throat, aware that his temperature was rising fast. What a knockout! Nothing like the other applicants, who had been consistently dowdy and prim. This was more like it. A younger woman, with animated features, a bold fashion sense. A Mary Poppins of the nineties. This could be just the compromise he was looking for. "Please, come in." He eagerly stepped aside as she swished past him in an electrically charged cloud of jasmine perfume.

"I probably should've called first."

Her voice was as sweet and light as her scent, yet laced with bravado. But that was only for the good. Handling his manipulative family was no cakewalk. It would take someone with spirit. Steven wandered after her, completely entranced by her swinging walk, the shimmering braid nestled between her shoulder blades. She paused in the center of the sitting room, stripping away her coat to reveal a red satin blouse and black slacks that complemented her small hourglass figure. He stared at the perfect picture of femininity, contemplating what her hair would look like undone, fluffed around her heart-shaped face, and what her legs looked like beneath those baggy trousers.

"Mr. Sanders, are you with me?"

He started at the lyrical interruption. "Gladly with you and half expecting you."

"Ah, so you've seen the evening papers then."

It suddenly registered with Steven that she'd entered with a folded newspaper tucked under her arm. It was now lying on the chair where she'd draped her coat. Perhaps she was featured in the agency's advertisement. It would be a genius business move. And to think he was going to have a crack at her before the other prospective employers started lining up!

He gestured to a wing chair, then strolled round it, buying the time to gather his wits. His head was spinning with possibilities. He wanted to know all about her but didn't want to startle her by coming on too strong. It was only fair to treat her coolly and conservatively, just as he had the old bats before her.

"About the paper, Mr. Sanders—"

He waved a dismissive hand. "I take everything in print with a grain of salt—prefer to make my own judgments. Let's just start talking with a clean slate and get to know each other on our own terms. I'm sure we can reach a mutually satisfying agreement."

"Okay...." Tessa studied him warily. This was to be his sum total reaction to her publicity stunt gone wrong? He was expecting her and was looking forward to it! "I want to begin by telling you that my career means the world to me," she said with greater assurance and warmth.

He was visibly impressed. "As it should be. It's difficult to do your best unless you enjoy your job."

"Yes, right." As hard as Tessa tried, she couldn't begin to imagine this magnetic man having "girl trouble" bad enough to warrant his family's interference. True, he was probably turning on the charm full throttle to make amends for the inconvenience they'd caused her at the store, but he appeared poised and sincere by nature.

"You're staring at me, Miss Jones."

Tessa blinked and smiled. "Oh, sorry. I'm just a little dazed by everything. It's happened so fast, you see. Please call me Tessa."

Refreshingly candid, as well, he mused in approval, guessing she could make any truth go down with a spoonful of that sugar the children were always singing about. He could see her with them in his mind's eye, sharing picnics in Central Park and ice skating at Rockefeller Center. "So you're saying this is your first venture?"

Did it matter? Tessa wondered. Perhaps he wanted to blame the contest mishap on her inexperience. "In this particular field, yes. I don't dare blow it."

Steven could barely contain his excitement. What luck to have first crack at her!

"Naturally, I've done some apprentice work," she went on to say, "during and after university."

"So you have a full education?"

"Well, you need a good education for almost any job these days. But I knew I'd have to work up slowly, learn the ins and outs. And it's also a matter of being as ready as possible when the right opportunity comes along."

It sounded as though she'd scrambled for this interview. He had left quite a lot of information with the employment agency, facts about the children, relocating to New York, his novelty company. It was probably silly, but he felt flattered by her eagerness, a rare occurrence at his age. But then she had to be at least a decade younger than he was, and her enthusiasm did make him feel good. Was it true what they said about older men being susceptible to that kind of thing? Not him, though, he was too jaded. Most likely she simply appreciated a good deal when she saw it. Another attribute!

Steven stared out the window to conceal his smug expression. "So you think we can come to mutually acceptable terms?"

She nodded vigorously. "I do. That's why I came rushing over. As vague as your mother can be at times, she seemed certain that you'd be more than willing to see me."

Steven whirled, regarding her with a sagging jaw. "My mother? You discussed all this in advance with my mother?"

"I thought you knew. Millicent handpicked me personally, it seems. I tried to speak to her, but she only talks in circles, doesn't she. So it seemed smartest to work things out with you."

Steven marveled at Millicent's nerve. She must have marched down to the Bond Street agency and given Tessa a preliminary screening. It was obvious the others hadn't met her. This woman had to be Millicent's personal choice.

"You seem so surprised."

"I am a little. But I'm happy, too, Tessa. Mother will be a lot more cooperative if she approved of you herself."

Tessa squeezed the armrests of the chair. Why did he seem so downright delighted by it? Did he too believe she was part of the wedding package? No, he was far too smart to be part of his children's fantasy. Though it was rather fun to imagine herself as Steven Sanders's prize for just a brief moment in time.

"My mother can be pushy, and I don't always care for it, but this time she's done me a huge favor." He moved closer, resting his hands on the arms of the chair so their faces were almost touching. "As a matter of fact, I'd like to tie you up right now if you're willing."

Tessa's small body stiffened in the huge chair. "Tie me up?"

"Yes, don't you think that's a fair request? And a compliment?"

Tessa's gaze shifted round the room, as she pondered her escape. "I guess I misread your signals."

"Believe me, this is how it's generally done, Tessa, at least in America. I can't go to bed tonight on a maybe." His expression grew earnest and his voice dropped to a rasp. "I have to take action before you walk back out that door. Before the kids return."

"You expect a bit on the side, on top of all the rest?" She gasped in dismay.

Steven reared back suddenly, as though the chair were on fire. "You don't think I meant tie you up literally!"

"Well, no," she mumbled, a telltale flush giving her away. "So... what did you mean?"

She looked ready to kill, but he couldn't help the amused grin tugging at his lips. How naive could she be! "I'm talking about signing an agreement. Nothing fancy, just an outline of our mutual expectations. I could send for a clerical worker—I have connections in the city...."

Tessa listened to his patient, pandering explanation, all the while feeling her temper on the boil. She'd come over here, ready to offer him a mock engagement as a means out of this mess, and all he seemed able to do was further complicate the predicament they were in. "It seems totally absurd to me that you need a written agreement for a simple little engagement. After all, my word is good. And besides, there isn't much else I can give you, is there. You already have my delicate reputation in your hands. The way I see it, your family's set me up and you have a duty to bail me out. If I don't need a contract, then you don't—"

"Simple little engagement?" He plucked those three words out of her speech on a lethal note. "As in marriage?"

Tessa jumped to her feet, appearing a lot taller than five foot three. "I thought you understood. What else could I possibly want from you!"

Steven exhaled in disappointment. This was just another of Millicent's attempts to marry him off. The details didn't really matter. All he knew was that for a few glorious minutes he'd believed he'd found the answer to his prayers, to his children's needs. With ill-concealed fury, Steven stalked over to retrieve her coat from the opposite chair, holding it open for her.

Tessa refused to acknowledge the gesture and faced him with her arms at her sides. She couldn't imagine what had come over him all of a sudden. His expression had closed up completely, and to her chagrin, she experienced a sense of loss. She'd liked the Steven Sanders who'd turned on the dazzle. "Where did I go wrong?"

"When you got into cahoots with my meddling mother!"

"Not cahoots—she did it all! Didn't you notice how shocked I looked?"

"When?"

"In the newspaper!"

He turned then to retrieve the section of paper that had slipped off her coat to the floor. There were his children on the front page in a cartoonlike pose with Tessa, his daughter clinging to her like a newly won trophy, his son and heir holding up her skirt to take a peek beneath it.

"You're a DeWilde employee?" he asked hoarsely.

"Yes."

"I thought you were here for the nanny position."

"Me? Are you out of your mind? I don't know the first thing about caring for children."

He was openly dumbfounded. "Well, you could've fooled me."

"I did fool you." And it felt mighty good after that tie-up mistake.

He scanned the article beneath the photograph, raw fear filling his face. "This does talk of marriage! Between you and me—me and you!"

She didn't know whether to be amused or insulted by his open terror. "Slow down. You take news stories with a grain of salt, remember?"

"Yes. Usually. But this one is about me." The paper shook in his hand. "About solid plans! Millicent's outdone herself!"

"I'm sure she has. But you aren't snared, not really. Look here." She moved his finger to the center column. "It says that I'm a designer struggling to make the big time, a career girl with goals. Believe me, the last thing I want or need is a ready-made family. I love being single. Absolutely adore it!" She gave his solid shoulder a shake. "You're safe, man, safe from the jaws of matrimony!"

Quite pale now, Steven rested his elbow on the top of a wingback chair and read the entire article with care. It explained about the essay contest and the wedding package prize, and even included the plea written by his precocious children.

"Guess I should apologize for my family," he grumbled. "I don't know why they've gone to such lengths to win you—"

"Thanks a heap!"

"Uh, sorry again."

"I think there are reasons why they found me so irresistible, the perfect bride for you." His blank look would have sent a lesser woman into fits. "Put it all together," she coaxed. "Poor unmarried shopgirl. Prince of a father. A peek at my feet. I'm Cinderella—your fairy-tale partner come to life!"

"Oh, yes." He frowned. "You seem bright enough. Why didn't you try and put a stop to all this?"

"It's hard to think when all the cameras and reporters are crowding in on you—and someone is baring your assets."

He gazed at the photo, appreciating her shapely legs. "I suppose it would be."

"Under the circumstances, don't you think you owe me some help out of this mess?"

"Ah, the reason you've come in the first place, I suppose." He stroked his chin. "Let's see, what's fair...."

She clasped her hands together eagerly. "I would appreciate your input. Honestly."

"Hey, I know. I'll decline the prize," he offered lavishly, as though presenting her with the keys to his kingdom. "DeWilde's can award the wedding package to another entrant. In return for the favor, you can agree to a retraction."

"But I don't want a retraction!"

He was openly perplexed. "You don't want to get married. You don't want a retraction. Just what do you want, Miss Jones?"

Miss Jones again? Tessa shook her head. He wasn't going to backtrack now, try to inject some formality into this situation, was he? Not after his own son had pulled up her skirt! "What I want, Steven, is something in between." He actually gulped, like a frightened boy. If he could see himself through her eyes, his self-image would never be the same! She controlled her twitching mouth. "Now, don't go panicky again. You know there is a vast difference between agreeing to marriage and truly being married."

"It's one measly step."

"In our case it'll be an entire ocean. Millicent said you'd be here only a week. Pretend for that short span of time that we're engaged and you'll be off the hook."

He raised his palms in defense. "Oh, no."

"Even if it's the only way you can really help me? The only way I can save my job? My superiors are very unhappy. It's bad enough that an employee like me—no matter how unwitting—is a recipient of the prize, especially when the contest was my idea. But even worse, they fear that DeWilde's dignified reputation will be damaged if it leaks out that we're strangers, set up by two children."

"I might be able to get you another position at another store," he suggested. "Would that repair the damage my family's done?"

As if she could go work for a DeWilde competitor! Of course, how could he know about her family connection to the store? "I'm not the only one set to lose," she told him. "The futures of other designers are at stake here, too. If this contest fails, there won't be any more contests.''

"Wouldn't it have been wise to give me a call yesterday, before the announcement, just to make sure that the daddy in question was in the market for a wedding?''

His point was valid, of course. "You're absolutely right. It just didn't occur to anyone, this being a trial promotion and all.''

He shook his head. "I happen to be in the middle of a very delicate business negotiation. I can't afford this distraction.''

"According to your family, you have no one else who matters,'' she wheedled sweetly. "The week will be over before you know it. You can fly back to the States and I'll announce our breakup in due course.''

He couldn't help but admire her chutzpah. She'd expected to just waltz in here and finagle the matrimonial package out of him! It hadn't been his style in recent years to confide his real feelings to anyone, but he didn't know any other way to put the brakes on this captivating steamroller.

He studied his blunt fingernails, avoiding her vivid green eyes. "As you've no doubt gathered by the essay, I was widowed relatively young.''

"Yes. I'm as sorry as I can be about that.''

"My wife had a weak heart, caused by a bout of rheumatic fever as a child. She was barely thirty at the time. It was all very hard to take, and I'm very set on remaining single. It's my goal to convince the kids that they can lead a happy life without a replacement mother.''

"This isn't a real life commitment,'' she protested. "It's just a few days out of your life!''

"I'm thinking especially of Natalie and Nick, and their attachment to you. It would be devastating for them to lose you when the week was up. It seems best to me if you leave now, before they return."

Tessa sighed as she thought of the bubbly pair. "And never see them again? They adore me. They think I belong to them."

"But you don't," he argued. "Your hanging around would just encourage more false hope. And I'm hoping this mix-up will cure my mother's meddling once and for all," he confided with a wicked gleam. "She can explain to the press and everyone else that it was all a mistake."

"Can't you cure her next time?"

"No. She might not make the papers next time."

Tessa sighed doubtfully. "It just might work by putting the brakes on Millicent's games for good. But I must warn you that those children are still going to want a new mum."

Steven smiled tightly, fuming at her nerve. "You speak like a parent with experience, Miss Jones."

"No, I'm a child with experience, Steven. One who lost her mum quite young in a light plane crash over the Greek islands. My father never remarried, you see, and it was a tough go. I still . . . well, I still search out mother figures. Hard as I've tried to get over it, there's a tiny little girl inside me who wants that kind of affection. There's a uniqueness to the bond."

Steven could tell the admission was a tough one for her. He appreciated her honesty, but it scared him all the more. They'd barely met and yet were opening up the way people do when they're instantly attracted to each other. He simply had to get rid of her fast. "I'm sorry you were dragged into our affairs, but I think a clean break is the best," he said evenly. "You make amends to your employer and I'll take care of my family. Though, if you like, I could speak to your boss," he said as an afterthought. "Explain about my mother..."

"He already got a good dose of Millicent," Tessa cut in sharply. "That's doing a whole lot of nothing."

"I apologize. Good—" Steven whisked open the door, only to find his family on the other side, carrying sacks from a variety of shops.

"How nice!" Millicent greeted the startled couple. "Everybody's been shopping for what they need today, it seems."

Nicky and Natalie's small mouths opened wide at the sight of their father with the mother of their dreams.

"She's here," Nicky breathed reverently.

Natalie's shiny eyes shifted to her father. "Isn't she perfect for us, Daddy? She even comes with her own dress and party shoes and everything!"

CHAPTER FIVE

"TESSA WAS JUST LEAVING," Steven announced in his strongest fatherly tones as Nicky and Natalie converged on him in a chorus of groans. Millicent shut the door behind them with a thump, leaning against it with an armload of newspapers identical to the one Tessa had brought along. The older woman sagged, as though dead on her feet, but her mission now seemed to be blocking the exit.

"She can't go yet, Daddy," Natalie protested, curling her little fingers around his belt. "You tell her to stay. You're her new prince. She'll listen to you."

Steven flushed. "Honey, honey, slow down. Tessa's told me everything, and we really have to talk it over."

Tessa stood by passively, infuriated with Steven's decision not to help her but sympathizing with his discomfort just the same. This particular mix-up had to be a dandy of a challenge—how to break the truth to them without causing complete devastation. To believe she had won a mother, only to lose her, would have destroyed Tessa emotionally at Natalie's age. As Steven slipped a finger behind the tight knot in his red tie, she gasped for some extra air herself.

"Are we getting married today?" Nicky asked, his innocent eyes sparkling. "Don't forget the cake. Chocolate fudge would be real good."

Natalie turned to her brother with a tolerant smile. "Chocolate fudge was fine for your birthday, but Daddy's cake will probably be white. With lots of flowers to match the flower girl dress." She touched the bodice of her own frilly blue frock as her eyes sought Tessa's. "You think about a flower girl yet?"

Tessa instinctively took a step back. "No, I haven't."

"Natalie wears pink very well," Millicent gushed, unobtrusively raising a hand to slide the safety chain on the door in place. "As do I."

"Mother!" Steven's voice was weighted with anger and amazement. "We've taken up enough of this lady's time. She has a life of her own, things to do. It's time to step aside. Literally!"

Nicky folded his arms across his chest and scrutinized his father. "Did you make her mad? After all we done for you?"

"Of course not!" Tessa smoothly interceded. "We've had a very interesting chat."

"Then why are you going, princess mommy?" Nicky sidled up to her and tipped his head against her sleeve with a wistful sigh.

She gave his blond head an awkward pat, gazing at his father. "I suppose I could stay on for a little while, Steven, and help you explain."

Steven slipped off her coat, his features brightening with a new light that made her muscles melt. "Thanks," he murmured close to her ear. "I appreciate it."

Her green eyes twinkled with a stubborn glitter. "I'm doing it just for them."

"Makes it even nicer."

He was making a huge concession, she realized, walking straight into a very uncomfortable family trap. Apparently this man's greatest weakness was his pair of little powerhouses. She felt her irritation ebbing away. "Ooh, how I was enjoying working up a burn over you!"

His mouth curved deliciously. "I know."

Natalie took Tessa's hand and led her back to the sitting area. "That's a lovely coat. Purple is one of my new favorite colors."

Tessa sat down on the settee, tensing as if she were sinking into quicksand. The Sanderses, on the other hand, seemed far more relaxed, convinced their trap for her was secured. Giggling, Natalie bounced down beside her. A furtive Nicky raced off to the bedroom. And Millicent dared to leave her sentry post, her thin shoulders thrown back as though the weight of the world had suddenly been lifted from them.

"Afraid Tessa's going to try and make a break for it, Mother?" Steven asked dryly as he released the security chain on the door.

"Steven, really," she reprimanded him, setting the stack of papers on the cherrywood desk with a thump. "What will Tessa think of me?"

"Oh, I imagine she's already figured you out."

Millicent's smile was beatific. "Oh, that would be convenient."

Steven sauntered over to the desk, his hands in his pockets. "Everything seems to be at your convenience around here. The contest, Tessa's surprise visit."

"I hope sending Tessa over during your interviews didn't pose a problem."

He raised his eyes to the ceiling. "Heck, no, I enjoyed mistaking her for an applicant and making a fool of myself."

Millicent's chin quivered in affront. "Impossible! A Sanders never plays the fool."

Steven glanced back at the settee just in time to catch a glimpse of Tessa's dancing green eyes before her lashes swept down. It seemed he was the only one who wasn't enjoying this disastrous mix-up on some level. He leaned over the desk until he was nose to nose with Millicent. "You went way too far this time," he muttered quietly.

She stared back at him guilelessly. "But how does a matchmaker measure these things? A dash of mischief, a dollop of instinct—"

"A cupful of nitro!" Steven's whisper grew hoarse. "Between your schtick at the store and my behavior here, Tessa Jones has been offended beyond reason. And now the children want her and only her—"

Millicent pressed a hand to his forehead. "You look strained, dear. It makes me wonder if this nanny search is simply too much—"

"It wouldn't be if you'd stop pushing potential wives on me." Steven was aware that Natalie and Tessa were leaning forward, straining to hear. He couldn't help but appreciate how cute the two of them looked, seated together, their eyes bright with interest. The picture looked too right for comfort.

"Now, Daddy, you couldn't find a bride on your own," Natalie scolded. "You know that."

Steven flushed with embarrassment. Leave it to his own child to reduce his complicated reasons for not remarrying to a simple case of complete incompetence. Would he have a smidgen of pride left in the end?

Millicent sniffed. ''The child's right. Time is ticking by and things get rusty if they're not used often enough.''

''Mother!'' Steven thundered in mortification.

''I'm referring to charm, Steven,'' she maintained calmly. ''The process of courting a woman properly. The rest can be done adequately by all God's creatures.''

Tessa's amusement did finally escape in a giggle then. She quickly pressed a finger to her mouth as Steven glared at her.

Nothing was rusty on him! The compulsion to prove it to this pretty woman swelled inside him like a mounting hurricane. But that was exactly what Millicent had hoped for, wasn't it?

A horrifying thought suddenly occurred to him. Had his meddling mother finally found him a suitable match? She'd done so poorly up until now that he hadn't concerned himself with the possibility of success. He'd focused on polite rejections, keeping the family name from humiliation, and all the while had managed to maintain a certain detachment from the women in question. And for all its discomfort, he'd been able to handle things with detached control. Until today. It seemed that for the first time he might be forced to work his way out of a genuine emotional entanglement.

''Are you mad at me, Daddy?''

Natalie's plaintive plea brought Steven's priorities back into line. He realized he was wearing a ferocious frown. ''No, honey,'' he hastened to assure her.

"I just feel that you're helping Daddy too much this time."

"No, I'm not," she insisted, clicking her heels in the air. "You can't find a new mommy yourself! You try and try and still are the old maid!"

"My dear, you're too young—"

"You always say I'm old enough for hard things!" she protested fiercely. "Like being the mommy of the house and helping Grandma. I can't do it all by myself! I need help!"

Tessa's arm automatically curved around Natalie's slender shoulders and she rocked her gently. "Surely your father doesn't expect you to do all the things an adult does."

As kind an act as it was, it threatened Steven at gut level. With every passing minute Tessa was becoming more indispensable. "A nanny will take over all the big responsibilities," he promised, squeezing his daughter's flying shoes.

Her small face was pinched with determination. "We won Tessa fair and square."

"You can't win a person. The idea is ridiculous. Isn't the idea ridiculous, Miss Jones?"

"I suppose you can win a person's heart," she protested.

"Have I managed to win yours?" he asked, to clarify.

She smiled flirtatiously. "Well, I'm not sure you had the time...."

Steven's jaw tightened. She was thinking it over! "Careful how you answer, Tessa. Things are taken quite literally around here. My children believe they've won you from head to toe, heart included."

Tessa was instantly contrite. "Oh, I see where you're going. Your father's right, Natalie, you can't win another person. And I told you as much back at the store, didn't I?"

Steven raised a finger. "We're missing someone. Nicky, come here!"

Nicky bounded out of the bedroom, all smiles.

"Good boy." Steven favored his son with a determined smile, beckoning him closer.

Nicky fidgeted from foot to foot, obviously concealing something behind his bulky red sweater.

Steven touched his son's shoulder. "Now, Tessa explained to me about you mistaking her for Cinderella. She is not—"

"I know, Daddy," Nicky chirped, offering Tessa a wrinkled-nose grin.

"Really?"

"Sure," Natalie agreed. "We made a mistake about it. She had both her shoes all the time, under her dress."

"I peeked inside her dress," Nicky proudly confided, man to man.

Steven shook his head. An irresistible fantasy for any man large or small! "So you understand then that she's a regular person."

Nicky frowned in uncertainty. "Have you got a mother?" he asked Tessa.

She cleared her throat. "No, as it happens, I don't."

"Got a castle?"

"I'm afraid I live in a flat in Battersea."

"I bet it's up high," Nicky persisted. "With a garden."

"Yes—" She shifted slightly as Nicky moved in behind them.

"Rapunzel! Rapunzel! Let down your hair!"

At his command, Natalie tossed Tessa's thick burnished braid over the back of the settee. Tessa could feel Nicky's little fingers peeling off the binder that held her hair in place and suddenly remembered the fate of that heroine's mane. "Nicky," she said sharply. "What's hidden in your hand?"

Nicky rested his chin on Tessa's shoulder and reached round to show her a large golden comb. "It's Grandma's."

"Oh." Tessa sighed in relief, aware of his warm breath against her ear, the scent of his mild shampoo. She'd never had such close contact with children and was finding it rather nice. They kept a person on her toes, but their adoration was good for the ego. "That's all right, then. Comb away."

Steven was struck speechless by his son's clever maneuver. So determined to hold on to Tessa, Nicky had taken a detour into another tale entirely!

Tessa watched Steven lift his shoulders and rub his temples, as though trying to loosen up. He looked so lost and so endearing at that unguarded moment that she was tempted to curl her fingers around his tie, pull him down to her level and kiss him long and hard.

The idea startled her. By no stretch of the imagination could he be mistaken for the sort of devilishly carefree man she normally dated, the kind who would gladly indulge in a harmless engagement farce just for the adventure of it all.

So what was the attraction? Perhaps it was her affinity to the color red, displayed so prominently at the moment in his face and tie. Or maybe it was a simple case of being denied. Whatever it was, the next move had to be his. She'd made more than her share of advances. She couldn't take him on kicking and screaming, not even for the children's sake.

She gently took hold of her partially undone braid and stood up. "I really must be going. My landlady has some errands for me to run, and I have a sewing project in the works." She smiled down at Nicky and Natalie. "I think you've got the message that I'm truly not Cinderella or Rapunzel, haven't you?"

"But you could be any princess here!" Natalie bounced to her feet and scurried over to the desk. "See this phone?" She grabbed the black receiver in her hand and set it by her ear. "All we have to do is call up a number and order food. The cook down in the kitchen makes it and a butler in a nice red jacket brings it to the door."

"Room service, Natalie," Steven firmly corrected her, replacing the receiver in its cradle. "Plain old twentieth-century room service."

"And the upstairs maid comes every day and cleans up all the dirt. She wears a uniform and brings little soaps." She spread her arms wide. "It's really neat—and all for you!"

Steven's heart lurched as he watched the desperate display. And all this while he had believed his parenting methods were succeeding. He closed his eyes as a stark revelation struck him. He needed Tessa more than she needed him. He had all along but had refused to see it. She was in the driver's seat here, while he was grabbing hold of the back fender, trotting to keep up. And she was heading out the door right now at a brisk clip.

"Wait, Tessa!"

"Hurry, Daddy, hurry!" the small voices coaxed.

He barreled into the hallway, nearly colliding with Tessa, who'd paused to button her coat. She only looked up at him after carefully adjusting the strap of her shoulder bag. "I'm tired of going round with you."

His mouth curved up with a trace of cynicism. "Already? When we're about to be married?"

"You know what I mean. I didn't want to say anything in front of the kids—"

"What didn't you and my mother say!"

She made a disgusted sound. "You think you're a prize to deal with, treating marriage like the plague?" She tried to step away, but he snagged her elbow.

"Okay. I'll be a good sport about the engagement. I'll release a statement to the press if you want, speak to your employers—whatever it takes."

"And say the marriage was your idea," she added.

"Huh!"

"You have to take full responsibility for entering the contest, so it doesn't look rigged."

He exhaled noisily. "Okay, I'll do that, too."

Tessa's plan was preconceived, so her words flowed easily. "We'll keep details sketchy—say we met in New York last year while I was visiting the garment district."

"Fine, fine."

She tried to conceal her delight, but judging by his scowl, she had to look like a kitten before a bowl of rich cream.

"Don't look so smug. Your job isn't near finished, either."

"I'll be in touch with the children, of course."

"Very close touch! You'll have to show them your world, where you hang out when you're not up on that pedestal in a wedding gown. When we board that plane at Heathrow I want them to do so happily, without feeling that they've missed out on a fairy-tale mother."

"That seems like an awesome responsibility on my part."

"Yes, but it's part of the deal. I want a guarantee that the children will not be devastated when we leave without you."

Tessa shook her head slowly. What if she couldn't do it? What if she let them down somehow?

Natalie poked her head out the door. "There's a reporter on the telephone, Daddy."

"Thanks, baby. Tell Grandma I'm coming." He hovered over Tessa, his arms folded over his huge chest. The pressure had shifted to her now.

"I suppose we could spend some time together tomorrow," she said quickly. "It's Saturday. I could chauffeur you around the city, show you my flat."

"Eleven o'clock's good for us."

"Super. Now, get that call. Please!" She drew a hesitant breath as she grasped the doorknob. "I hope I can do this right."

He offered her a faint smile. "Start by reining in your charisma. They'll never let you go if you don't."

With a curt nod, Steven walked back into the suite. She absorbed the impact of his last statement. The words had been complimentary, but he had somehow twisted them so they felt anything but. Never in her entire life had she been so disgusted with a man and attracted to him at the same time!

Steven's feelings were running along a similar vein as he entered the hotel suite alone. Tessa was exactly the kind of woman he liked to date—independent, bright, career-minded, with no matrimonial expectations. Too bad he hadn't met her under different circumstances, apart from the children. There wouldn't be this pressure to make her part of the family. And she wouldn't have been desperate enough to come over with an offer bordering on blackmail!

He nearly tripped over the children as they waited inside the door, their faces turned up to him like bright sunflowers. He was touched and a little envious at their eagerness. "Everything's fixed. We're spending time with Tessa tomorrow." He returned their fierce squeezes, then followed the sound of Millicent's voice to his bedroom. She was poised at the nightstand, the telephone receiver held to one ear.

"Just one moment, here he is now." She cupped her hand over the mouthpiece. "It's a television reporter."

"Who called whom?"

"I wouldn't know his number."

"You know everybody's number." He rounded the bed and took the receiver. "This is Steven Sanders. Yes, I'm delighted with the outcome of the contest."

With an extravagant sigh, Millicent sank down on the edge of the neatly made bed, smoothing her purple pajamas.

"No, of course it was all on the up and up. Tessa wasn't involved in our entering at all. My children won the contest fair and square. No one was more surprised than the bride. Of course she's accepted our proposal! My children can be persuasive, as everyone at DeWilde's must know by now. No, we haven't set a date. Tessa is still reeling in surprise. We met in New York last year. I live there. Yes, I am Sanders Novelties. Look, that's all there is to tell at this point. You're welcome. Goodbye."

Steven hung up the telephone and turned to find Millicent's hands clasped over her lips, which she was obviously trying to keep from trembling. "It's not for real, Mother."

"But you liked her, I could tell."

"Yes, she's very lovely."

"Natalie and Nicky were instantly taken with her, too."

Steven shrugged. "She relates to them without even realizing it. But that might be mainly because of her own youth."

"I see what you're doing. You're using her age as an excuse for everything, for her appeal to the children, her unsuitability for you."

"Definitely," he easily admitted. "Her lack of experience with children *and* relationships puts us all on shaky ground."

Millicent's eyes gleamed shrewdly. "She seems more than capable of handling herself."

Steven chuckled as he remembered her expression when she thought he wished to tie her up.

"Don't hurt her now, Steven. I feel responsible for her—"

"Yes, you are." He sat down beside her on the floral spread and reached over to the nightstand for a pen and pad of paper. "But I'm going to help. Now then, if there are any more calls, I want you to stick to these statements. I know they're short, but any embellishing will cause Tessa more trouble—which she doesn't deserve."

"Have you noticed how much you care about her feelings?"

"Hard to tell under all this duress." Steven finished writing with a flourish and set the tablet in his mother's lap. "Someday I'll find a way to bottle your wiles and turn the tables."

Millicent laughed. "Not in this lifetime."

He was exasperated by her lack of remorse. "You should be ashamed of this stunt, Mom. You know my plate is full with business."

"I didn't expect this big hoopla, honestly. I simply wanted you to meet her."

"But why her? If you can't control yourself, why not pick on an anonymous clerk at Harrods or a waitress down in the hotel restaurant? Somebody miles from the spotlight?"

Millicent inhaled sharply as the truth nearly popped out. She had no right to reveal her reasons. Tessa seemed to be making an admirable attempt to succeed without resorting to family connections, and Millicent didn't want to upset her plans. Besides, Steven didn't deserve another lever to use against the girl. Knowledge was power and he seemed to have more than his share. Tessa was already vulnerable to him. Her vivid green eyes held the same glimmer that her grandmother Celeste's had when she was infatuated. But unlike Celeste, this girl had her feet firmly on the ground. She had goals, ambitions. If only nature would take its course and she and Steven were willing to explore the possibilities.

She realized that Steven was waiting for an answer. He looked quite miserable. "I meant this all in fun, truly."

Steven rose from the bed, his hands clenched at his sides. "Really? I can't help but feel that I'm losing ground with my own children. Their heads were turned so quickly and completely by this stranger!"

"How silly! Those rascals adore you. If you don't think so, page through our stacks of photo albums, run our videos once we're back home. It's all recorded in vivid color, the ski trips to Aspen, the tour through Disney World, the Rocky Mountain retreat. Not to mention the holidays and the parties to mark everything but a sneeze. And all of this is backed up by your accessibility, Steven. You're never out of their reach, even when you have to be away, and you're never stingy with your affection. The story is all there to read in their bright faces."

"Then why do they want to include Tessa so badly?" he asked bleakly.

"The maternal yearning is natural. And they believe they're helping you, as Natalie so bluntly pointed out a little while ago. You couldn't find a bride on your own, remember?"

"She made me look like a complete bungler. But I'm single by choice!"

Millicent made a clicking sound with her tongue. "You'd better be very careful about expressing that policy too strongly. The children just might end up with the idea that you don't value the bond of marriage anymore. A fine example that would make."

Steven flexed his fingers with deliberate concentration, struggling to keep his tone level against his rising emotions. "Nobody understands the value of marriage better than I. The trauma of Renee's passing still haunts me every day. Was there a way to save her from that heart attack? I can't stop wondering."

Millicent chose her words carefully, as she always did on this touchy subject. "Renee's time in our lives was far too short. But dwelling on the might-have-beens is not going to bring her back. It's time to let go. Time to open up to new options."

His voice shook a little, but the depth of his resolve obviously still reached to the pit of his soul. "I don't want to replace her, Mother."

"I will never give up, not until you're happy again."

"I am happy enough with my children, Mother, so your quest is a futile one." With a kiss to her forehead, he strode out of the room.

STEVEN SAW THE CHILDREN through supper, a second tumbling match on the floor and some television programs before tucking them into bed. By ten o'clock he was in a taxi, set for some adult fun with his friend and ally in the Butler Toys camp, Barry Lambert. The plan included a little handball at Barry's Soho gym, followed by a little shoptalk at his favorite neighborhood pub. Steven was looking forward to forgetting all about the feisty, persuasive Tessa Jones for a while.

But the jolly Barry wasn't about to let the De-Wilde headlines go by without some explanation. Once they were settled in for their post-game feast of fish and chips and ale, he wasted no time in producing a newspaper.

Steven munched on a chip in the noisy pub, annoyed with Barry's mocking attitude. "Well, I'm not free to come clean with the facts, but did you have the impression that I was here chasing a woman?"

"Not one particular woman," he teased, dousing his chips with vinegar.

"And do you see my style in that winning essay?"

"I suppose the wording is a bit simple for you."

"Well, add my matchmaking mother to the picture and it's easy to see what happened."

Barry took a draw from his heavy glass mug. "Ah, so it's a trap, then. I must say, though, this Tessa Jones is smashing. Nice legs."

Steven frowned as Barry ogled Tessa's photograph, resisting the urge to cover her exposed thighs with his hand. "She's not your type."

Barry's pale mustache seesawed playfully. "Oh, really? How can you be sure?"

"Because she's younger and gentler than the women you set us up with last night."

"I happen to be a very flexible guy."

Steven wondered if Barry was picturing Tessa in his bed and was relieved he had no way of knowing.

"You're wild for her," Barry observed suddenly with a wagging finger.

Steven stared down at his plate. An impetuous designer in her twenties was making him feel like a lusty teenager, and it appeared to be written on his face for all to see. "Eat your fish."

Barry shrugged in confusion. "Can't say I understand what's stopping you."

Steven smiled thinly. "No, I'm sure you can't."

"Never mind. I was only trying to lighten you up before we moved on to business."

"Trouble with Franklin Butler?"

"'Fraid so, chap. He and the board had a brief discussion after you left and the news isn't the best."

"He's decided against purchasing the Ranger rights?"

"Not exactly. He and the other members—who, by the way, miraculously always seem to agree with him—feel your Galaxy Rangers lack a certain charm."

"The hell they do! Every kid in America loves them."

"A point I hastened to make. Which is perhaps why I'll never make it to the namby-pamby board of directors."

Steven nodded in understanding. One thing he'd instantly liked about Barry when they'd first met in New York several months ago was the fact that he wasn't afraid to state and stand by his own opinions, no matter how unpopular they might be to senior management. A self-centered dandy, perhaps, but his own man just the same.

"It seems we have no choice but to strap ourselves to the drawing board and toss around ideas to make the Rangers more appealing."

Steven pushed his plate away, no longer hungry. "I can't tomorrow, not until five at the earliest."

"Why not? What could be more important?"

"I'm spending the day with Tessa and the children."

"Whatever for, if you're not pursuing her?"

"It's all in that newspaper article. My kids have it in their heads that Tessa's a fairy-tale princess and belongs to us. I have to straighten that out before we return home."

"One kiss to a frog like you should be proof enough. You're bound to stay an old croaker."

"Wish I'd thought of that test."

"I bet you do," Barry wagered with a conspiratorial wink.

Steven was visibly flustered over the thought of a mere kiss! "I just mean that maybe the whole situation could have been handled in a quicker, simpler way."

"Right. We'll work the evening shift instead. Don't worry yourself."

"Thanks, pal. It almost makes up for my letting you win tonight."

"What?" Barry lunged over the tippy wooden table, grabbing playfully at his friend's shirt. "You know I'm the better sport. Girls, games, you name it!"

Despite the gloomy situation, Steven couldn't help but laugh. But one thing Barry wouldn't get his hands on was Tessa.

CHAPTER SIX

"GOOD MORNING, Mr. DeWilde! Such a pleasure to see you." Shirley Briggs waved cheerily to Gabe Saturday morning from the window display she and her designers were in the process of redecorating. "We're working like fiends to finish up before the customers arrive." Brushing past her busy protégées, Shirley scampered for the three stairs leading out of the boxed-in area, stumbling a bit as she bent over to push her coffee and Danish out of sight behind a piece of trellis.

Gabe had no choice but to catch her round the fleshy waist as she missed the second step. Tessa, along with her co-workers Denise and Helen, shared a nudge and a silent laugh at their manager's expense.

Gabe righted Shirley on the floor as swiftly as possible, then turned his attention to the work in progress. As was customary, the windows were papered over for privacy from sidewalk gawkers. Tessa and the others were carefully arranging formally dressed female mannequins in a semicircle against some artificial shrubbery. Although DeWilde's had a director of visual merchandising whose staff usually dressed the store's windows, the designers in the Experimental Boutique had opted to do their own windows until they had established a firm direction and identity for the boutique.

Shirley inched up to Gabe, her brown eyes as hungry as a puppy's. "Even though it's still chilly February, we have to start thinking spring, spring, spring!"

"Oh, yes." Gabe kept staring straight ahead, hoping to discourage her.

"We've come up with a brainstorm, I think," Shirley confided. "A silk crepe cocktail dress that will go anywhere and do anything long after the big day. Practical, sophisticated, reasonably priced. It seems just the thing for the Experimental Boutique."

Gabe inspected the colorful array of dresses from a distance. "The bride's dress still manages to stand out, despite the fact that it's the same style as the others."

"We deliberately chose a uniquely fluorescent fabric for the bride, a whiter than white that's guaranteed to make her the center focus."

Gabe nodded in approval. "I like the concept."

"We're most proud, aren't we, ladies?"

Tessa and her companions offered him perfunctory nods. Gabe understood. Shirley was loosely throwing her "we" around again. He'd seen this idea outlined on Tessa's sketch pad weeks ago.

"We hope to have everything in place by opening time." Shirley glanced at her watch. "Many working girls bring their mums in on Saturday morning."

Hoping to shake her loose so that he could have a word with Tessa, Gabe wandered over to the remnants of the contest display stacked off to the side near the fitting rooms.

"Don't concern yourself about that, sir," Shirley cooed, still on his trail. "Stock is sending someone in to haul it downstairs."

"Good. On to new projects."

"Such a shame about Tessa Jones taking first place yesterday," she persisted. "You'd think her fiancé would have better sense than to enter an employee that way. You'd think she'd have warned him."

"How could she when she wasn't even expecting him in town?" he reasoned. Tessa had called him yesterday after her meeting with Steven Sanders and filled him in on their agreement. The story that Steven had rushed in with a surprise proposal seemed perfect, clearing suspicions of any contest fixing and giving Tessa a way out of the engagement once Steven was gone again. She could simply say she'd had second thoughts and turned him down.

"It still all seems rather irresponsible."

"The man meant no harm. Everything's been fixed." He fired the information at her at a clipped pace, leaving no room for further discussion. "Personnel has already contacted another winner—the Chelsea woman with the sailor boyfriend. Press releases have been issued." With that pointed dismissal, he turned to inspect the discarded banners stenciled with the prizes—Hawaiian Honeymoon, Flowers by Georges, Music by Max Sutton, and so on. He smiled as he envisioned those darling children clinging to his mortified cousin. Despite the inconvenience to the store, it had felt good to see Tessa shaken up a bit. She was so headstrong, so independent, so set in her ways. She'd yet to have an exclusive relationship where one was forced to compromise. But all good things eventually came to pass, and Gabe had the feeling that Tessa was on the brink of one of life's greatest adventures.

"Well, if there's nothing else I can do for you, Mr. DeWilde..."

Gabe turned, noting the unrelenting hope in Shirley's eyes. "I'd like to speak to Miss Jones, if you can spare her."

"Certainly." Mistakenly anticipating a dressing-down for her subordinate, she clattered back toward the window, exuberantly calling Tessa's name.

Tessa joined Gabe near the pile of discarded display material, fluttering her lashes with feigned innocence. "Why weren't you on hand to catch me off the stairs, as well?"

His hazel eyes danced merrily. "I suppose you wish I'd let her take the fall."

"I think she'd have landed on her feet one way or the other." She kept her stature stiff, as would be expected of a subordinate, but her eyes sparkled saucily. "What do you want? It's my day off, you know, and I'm frightfully busy—saving the store from humiliation and all."

"First off, I want to remind you to give me back the pearls for safekeeping. It's been an agonizing week for me, knowing they're out in the open someplace in your flat."

"They happen to be safe and sound in my jewelry—safe."

He arched his brows in doubt. Chest of drawers was more like it.

"I'll bring them along to the Savoy tomorrow, I promise. If that dinner invitation is still on."

"It is," he quickly assured her. "Father needs a diversion and you're the biggest one I can think of."

"Thanks... I think."

"If you like, I could swing by later for the neck-lace."

"No! Today's not good."

"Oh, right. You're picking up the Sanders crew, aren't you?"

"How do you know?"

"I got a call from your Steven last night."

Her mouth sagged open. "My Ste— He's not mine! And why should he call you, anyway?"

He leaned against the wall, folding his arms across his chest. "He didn't ring me up personally. He called the corporate line. Monica, Father's secretary, spoke to him. Since she knew that I was the manager responsible for the contest, she routed it on to me."

"So what more did he want? The prizes shipped to New York? A garter for his trophy case?"

"He merely wanted to make sure your job was secure."

"Oh." She grew sheepish. "That was a kind gesture."

"I thought so. When he first began talking along the lines of your employment, I thought he was going to ask me to fire you."

"He wouldn't! He's far too..." Her face softened as she tried to put her feelings into words. "Fair-minded."

"Anger and affection all rolled into one?" Gabe stroked his jawline thoughtfully. "I can't remember any man ever catching you on both fronts. Could be something's brewing."

"He only sees me as a distraction to his kids. Hard to believe, isn't it? I've been desired in many different ways, but as a motherly role model?" Her face puckered in distress. "It's my one weak area. The part of myself I doubt."

Gabe smiled encouragingly. "Think of it as the ultimate adventure. You're the girl who likes to wake up each morning, unsure where the day will take her."

She resisted the childish urge to give the lock of hair resting on his forehead a very painful yank. "I could gleefully wallop you right now."

Gabe adjusted his striped tie with a haughty look. "Such cheek. To think I begged you to join the DeWilde team. Why, you've been nothing but a nuisance."

"And right now I've got to run." She stepped into the entrance to the fitting room, quickly reappearing with a roomy denim jacket embroidered with bold flowers. She eased the jacket over her plum jeans and metallic top, then paused to check her reflection in one of the many full-length mirrors along the wall. She gave her loose hair a fluff.

He read the uncertainty in her eyes and smiled. "You look fine, you'll do fine."

"And if I have any problems?"

He waved with airy indifference. "Just give a call."

Her eyes crinkled affectionately. "Really?"

Gabe's shoulders shook with unreleased laughter. "Just call 999."

With a look certain to kill a lesser man, she stormed off into the unknown.

TESSA EASED HER SILVER Honda up to the entrance of the London Hilton to find the Sanderses ready and waiting on the sidewalk. They looked every bit the tourists. Steven had a camera looped round his neck and was staring off into the sky as if looking for the sun. Natalie was clutching a huge black patent leather handbag that had to be a discard of her grandmother's as she danced around on the sidewalk. And Nicky, his blond head bobbing every which way, was watching the trotting horses across Park Lane in Hyde Park. They were all dressed in drab earth-tone twills and functional all-weather jackets probably worth more than her clunky old car.

The vehicle had been a purchase from Mrs. Mortimer. Tessa needed something to complement her shopgirl life-style and Mrs. Mortimer needed cash for a newer, trustier sedan. The landlady had naively charged Tessa far more than the Honda was worth and she'd gladly given her the charitable boost. Once Tessa revealed her identity, she planned to help Mrs. Mortimer a whole lot more, shower the woman with the kind of favors she'd do for her own mother, were she alive.

Tessa shifted into neutral and checked her lipstick in the rearview mirror. What would Steven think of her bold style? She was going to look like a neon sign standing up beside them. But wasn't it rather symbolic, considering how different their lives were? The free-spirited artist versus the corporate male, their only common link two children with an outrageous tale to tell.

And what did those children say about the man? Though mischievous, they showed all the qualities of a solid upbringing, confidence, intelligence and a sense of humor. Obviously, Steven Sanders had done a lot of things right.

Damn, no matter how hard she tried, she couldn't shake the feeling that beneath the conservative exterior was an ever so sexy male! When he spoke, his words might seem uptight, but his delivery, with that whiskey-rough voice of his...

The passenger door popped open and he peered in at her with a friendly smile. "Hello. How are you?"

"No rain today, it seems. What luck!" She groaned inwardly. A mere smile from him and all she could think to talk about was the bloody weather!

If Steven noticed her discomfort, he didn't show it. He was far too busy strapping his precious cargo into the back seat. She turned her gaze to the bustling Hyde Park, putting herself in the tour guide mode.

"What happened to your hair?" Natalie asked.

Tessa shifted on the seat to find the two small faces set in betrayal. "It's loose, that's all."

Nicky moaned in disappointment. "It's different. I don't like it."

Steven eased in front beside Tessa, giving her knee a pat. "It's a wonderful change. As is the getup."

Getup? Did he think she was in costume? This was the real her!

It was tough to stay insulted, though, when his roving eye gleamed with a basic male appreciation. She pulled out into traffic with a tingling awareness and the hope that he just might see her as something other than an inconvenience.

Always more comfortable when she was talking, Tessa drove about pointing out interesting sights. She deliberately took the route through Piccadilly Circus, circling round to show them how the five streets connected and where the statue of Eros stood. The children oohed and aahed over the figure of the archer and asked Tessa who he was.

She opted for the simplest explanation. "He's known as the god of Love."

"I'll bet even he's married, Daddy," Natalie mumbled into Steven's ear.

Steven chuckled, half turning to squeeze the small hand on his shoulder. "If he isn't, I'm sure you could set something up."

Everyone laughed then, the mood in the car growing jolly. Tessa announced her plans to take them to the Bethnal Green Museum of Childhood. "It's a wonderful spot to take snapshots, Steven. And it's something the children will remember for years to come when the rest fades away."

Steven merely smiled, thinking that they'd probably remember Tessa and little else. She was just that captivating. And so damn tempting. But it would be wrong to get anybody's hopes up by showing signs of real interest. Steven didn't make promises he couldn't fulfill, and Tessa was still young enough to find hope in the smallest encouragements. He hadn't missed her admiring glances. She was considering her options.

They spent the next couple of hours in the Victorian building of glass and brick, taking in a children's show and examining a huge variety of antique soldiers, trains and dolls. There were board games on display, as well, which gave Steven the chance to make comparisons to his own work and explain how his grandfather had made his fortune creating games like these. When Nicky expressed an interest in viewing the trains and teddy bears in the lower galleries one more time, Tessa took charge of Natalie and steered her to the dollhouses.

A look at the fifty dollhouses in the Central Hall sent Natalie into a tailspin. With huge saucerlike eyes, she peered into the late nineteenth-century houses full of lavish, heavy furniture. "I wish I could climb right in there and play, don't you?"

Hoping to inject a dose of reality into their conversation, Tessa gestured to a smaller Victorian model. "This is the kind of house I live in." Natalie straightened up, watching her closely to see if she was joking. "It's true. I have a landlady named Mrs. Mortimer. She owns the house. And it's divided up into four smaller flats—apartments to you."

"Is she a witch?"

"Oh my, never! She is the gentlest, sweetest woman I know."

"Must be a fairy godmother, then."

"Natalie, really. She's not a character from a fairy tale—she's my landlady!" Tessa determinedly took her hand and guided her to the display of doll clothes. "Just look at these clothes. This is how I got my start, sewing for my dolls. I was just about your age. Aren't the wedding dresses especially lovely?"

Natalie scampered on ahead, her mane flying over her tan jacket. "Oh, yes. But not as pretty as your white dress, Your Highness." She stopped long enough to execute a little curtsey.

In frustration, Tessa caught hold of her by the shoulder and cupped her tiny chin in her hand. "We need to talk."

Natalie's eyes sparkled. "Is this one of those chinwags I heard about?"

"I guess you could say it's a most important chinwag."

"What's the matter? You look kinda mad."

Tessa led her over to a small bench near an exit. They sat together, Natalie's large purse wedged in the space between them. "Natalie, you know full well that I'm not royalty, don't you?"

She brightened. "Nicky thinks you are."

"Just between us girls now, do you think so?"

"Just between us? Like a secret you can never tell?"

"Exactly."

"Well, you sure could be. You're pretty enough."

"Now, poppet..."

"Okay, Tessa," she said on a small sigh. "At first, in the store, I thought maybe you were. England has lots of princes and princesses. And Grandma said you're very special."

"Did she?" Tessa frowned, wondering if Millicent knew more than she was letting on about her true identity.

"But then you said you weren't, and Daddy said you weren't, so I figured Grandma Milly went overboard again."

"I see."

"I'm pretending for Nicky now. He's very attached to you and really thinks you belong to us."

Tessa's face was pinched with concern. "Oh, dear."

"I have to look out for him and make sure he doesn't ever get too hurt. Grandma gets tired and lets him run wild sometimes."

"Then perhaps your father is right to hire a nanny."

Natalie's mouth curved sweetly. "A mommy would be better, don't you think?"

Tessa cleared her throat. "If your father were to fall in love, that could happen. He wouldn't be very happy if he married someone just to be your mommy."

Natalie patted her hand. "You've made him very happy."

Tessa chuckled. "I don't think so, love."

"Of course you have! He was singing in the shower this morning. He hardly ever does that. And he let us have waffles for breakfast, and he didn't even yell when we jumped on his bed to wake him up."

"He's only trying to make this trip fun for you."

"When he was supposed to be sketching out some new story ideas for the Rangers, he drew a picture that looked like you."

Tessa's pulse jumped. "What?"

"I told him it had your head and he got all red and flipped the page over."

So he was thinking of her. And thanks to his candid daughter, she'd found out. Oh, how she'd like to give the issue a little nudge. She was dying to experiment a bit, see how strong the chemistry was between them.

"Do you think it could happen, Tessa?"

Tessa blinked, refocusing on the child. "What?"

"That you might fall in love with Daddy and marry us!" she blurted out impatiently.

"You think big, don't you?"

"We don't have much time. We'll be gone in a week."

"I can't make any promises, but I'll tell you what I can do. I can be your friend."

She extended her lower lip. "That's not the same at all."

Tessa gently stroked her hair. "We would make great friends, I think. I understand some of what you're going through. I lost my mother when I was a little girl and I desperately wanted another one."

"Did you get one?" she asked eagerly.

"No, my father never remarried."

"Oh." Natalie's head drooped to her chest.

"Friends are wonderful, you'll see. They chat together and shop and share secrets. And they call each other on the telephone anywhere in the world."

"Daddy has an 800 number for all of us to use in New York," she confided with growing interest. "You can call me on that for free. Every day. Before school!"

Tessa laughed merrily. "Well, I'm sure something can be arranged. All I ask in return is that you start to cut back on the pretending and work with Nicky, begin to let him down easy."

"I'll try. But gee whiz, wouldn't it be easier to just get married to Daddy for real?"

Gee whiz, she was beginning to think so!

A SHORT WHILE LATER they drove back to Tessa's flat on White's Row, making only one stop for Chinese takeaway.

"Here we are, then." Tessa stopped in front of an impressive Victorian house, second from the corner. It was rich in detail, with a roomy porch, steeply pitched roof and a fan window over the front door. "The bay window up on the left is my part of the house."

Steven helped the children out of the car, all the while taking in his surroundings. The street was well kept, its houses turn-of-the-century charming. "An impressive gray lady."

Tessa came to stand beside him on the sidewalk, juggling the sack of food and her roomy tote in her arms. She gratefully allowed Steven to take the food.

"Until last week it was a faded green one. But Mrs. Mortimer, the owner, decided the place needed a facelift. The maroon trim was my idea."

"Very vivid choice."

"All my decisions are bold ones, it seems." With a quick wink she hustled the children up the cracked concrete walk.

Steven lagged a few steps behind, enjoying the view. Watching her small slender form glide beneath that baggy denim jacket of hers had been delicious torture for the past few hours. Her body language was sheer poetry, sexy, natural, as alive as her feisty temperament.

He shivered slightly despite the dry weather and the hot cartons of food under his arm. Never was his protective shield more important than today. Tessa Jones was the worst kind of threat to his single status, an honest-to-goodness working girl on the lookout for an honest man. Could he ever open himself up and fall in love again? Could he?

Tessa was leading the children up the creaky carpeted staircase as he moved inside the house to join them. Her voice blended musically with theirs as though they'd known one another forever.

She had a big heart. And big hearts were easily breakable. He'd do well to remember that.

Tessa hung her jacket on a peg inside the door and invited them to do the same. She then moved to the windows overlooking the front yard and pushed aside the polished cotton curtains to allow the afternoon sunlight to pour in. The children were soon at her heels, inspecting her work area. Her sewing machine, dressmaker's dummy, sewing chest and boxes of patterns and bolts of fabric were spread all over the place.

Steven set the sack of food on her small wooden dining table, thinking how bright and clean everything seemed.

Tessa noticed his interest and instantly felt self-conscious about her cluttered digs. "I usually tidy up when I entertain and wrap a three-paneled screen around my workspace. But since you wanted the children to see things for real, I left everything in its natural state."

"It's very inviting."

She moved to a small cupboard beside the sink for plates. "Everything's old and worn. The furniture came with the place, you see. But I've had a lot of fun making new slipcovers and curtains, and adding rugs."

He nodded with approval. "You're very talented."

"I really enjoy the refurbishing process. Mrs. Mortimer gladly helped me out, leading me to bargains in the neighborhood shops. We're going to tackle her flat next." Tessa peered into the living room to find that the children were looking over her giant sewing chest, which sat on the floor near her machine. "You can look inside if you like. The top tray is all thread."

Steven had been hoping for the chance to discuss Millicent, and this seemed like an opening to work her in. When Tessa turned back to him, he spoke up quickly. "My mother would've led you in the opposite direction," he said, "to the most expensive stores in London for ready-made things, just to get the job done."

Tessa went about setting the table, opening a drawer for utensils, reaching into another cupboard for glasses. "That is another way of life entirely. One that seems to suit Millicent rather well."

"Yes, she funnels all her creative energy into public relations. She views manipulation as her primary role."

"I noticed."

"She's always been quite an asset to the family business. Sanders Novelties had been doing well financially when she met Robert, my father. He and my Grandpa Gerald already had the market cornered on the game board business, along with other kinds of toys, but they did lack social connections."

"Something Millicent had?"

"Yes, as the daughter of a Boston banker, she had the connections and she knew how to use them. The rest you can probably guess. She gave the Sanderses social status, learned the business and went on to lead a very productive life."

Tessa's mouth turned down ruefully. "I'm not surprised. Only a seasoned manipulator could rig my contest so successfully."

"It's an incurable habit. She leaves the company to me now, but she can't seem to stop meddling on a social level."

"Why are you telling me this?"

He leaned against the wall and stared down at his feet. "So you see her as more than a silly old fool, I suppose. She's just so upset that I haven't found a replacement for Renee. She's so accustomed to controlling her family and making sure they're settled and content. My father adored being steered around. He knew he could come home from a hard day at work and she'd have his personal life all mapped out. I've never liked that arrangement myself. Renee and I had our own life in Connecticut before my dad was diagnosed with cancer. My career choice was law. I originally moved back to New York to help out on a temporary basis. Then Renee died and I was living with my mother again like the old days, depending on her help, dodging her ploys. Her protest against my plans to hire a nanny has been her topper. This time her scheme borders on the ludicrous.''

"I think I understand the big picture. And I appreciate your telling me.''

Steven offered her a contrite smile. "Will you accept my apologies on her behalf?''

"Yes. But I too have a confession to make. I really like Millicent.''

"After all she's done?''

"She means well, and a part of me is flattered that she found me appealing enough to go to all this trouble.''

Steven felt a rush of relief. So many things could have gone wrong here. His mother had lucked out this time—big time.

Tessa called Natalie and Nicky to lunch, lowering a carton of fried rice to give them a whiff of the fragrant steam. Steven realized that the situation was quickly becoming cozy, and all because of Tessa, with her warm ways and homey nest. She most likely would succeed in convincing the kids that she was for real. But what if they wanted her all the more because of it? To Steven, the real Tessa was the most irresistible of all!

He started as he felt a tug on his belt loop. "Guess what, Daddy?" Natalie asked, her face aglow. "Tessa doesn't have a mommy, either. Isn't that sad?"

"She looks like she's made it just fine."

"Oh, but I think if sad people get together, they can be really happy."

Steven rubbed his hands together, pretending not to notice the yearning in Natalie's eyes. "Let's eat!"

Tessa used the mealtime to explain about all her tools. She told them that for weeks the dressmaker's dummy had worn the wedding dress they'd won at the store. The children were an avid audience, asking questions about her projects.

When they'd finished eating, Tessa sat cross-legged with them round the sewing box, lifting trays of gadgets out for their inspection, generously detailing the purpose of each one. Their fresh minds could only absorb so much, however, and they began to get restless. Since she was running out of steam herself, Tessa was more than happy to give them permission to inspect her small, modest bedroom at the end of the hallway. Natalie led Nicky by the hand, her huge black handbag bouncing between them.

Steven, in the meantime, had spent his time cleaning up the kitchen, even washing her breakfast dishes with the others. He peered out of the nook once the children were out of range, his expression tender and appreciative. "You've been great."

Tessa smiled over the lid of her sewing box. "So have you. Those dishes would've sat for hours."

"Almost finished."

Tessa watched as he disappeared back into the kitchen. Feeling playful, she decided to put his self-control to the test. She stretched out on the floor, arms over her head, and closed her eyes. Fluffing her long, thick hair around her head, she began purring like her landlady's large ginger cat. To her delight, it brought Steven racing out of the kitchen with a tea towel in his hands.

Tessa fluttered her lashes, pretending to be surprised to find him standing over her. He actually looked like a fairy-tale prince, towering over her, handsome, interested. He was so damn interested that he was trembling and kept wiping his huge hands in her tiny pink tea towel over and over again.

"Sorry if I startled you."

His gaze was hooded. "Liar."

She rose with a fluid dancer's grace and stood on tiptoe before him. He instinctively took a step back. "What are you so bloody scared of?" she asked.

A red tide of anger washed his features. "Do I look scared?"

Her green eyes twinkled with merriment. "Frightfully scared. Frightfully frightful."

Steven cradled her head in the tea towel, drawing her face close to his. The movement happened so quickly, it caught her off guard.

"What are you doing?"

He brushed her nose with his. "Maybe I'm trying to scare you back."

"Ah," she sighed, "now we're going places."

CHAPTER SEVEN

TESSA WAS JUST REACHING up to touch the planes of Steven's face when a sharp rap sounded on the door.

"I wonder who that could be?" Natalie trotted out of the bedroom with Nicky in tow, quaintly surprised that anyone would dare invade their small, isolated world. Steven shrugged innocently, tossing the tea towel to a chair as though it were incriminating evidence.

"Let's find out together," Tessa suggested brightly, smoothing her mussed hair. Before they could move, the door opened on its own.

"It's only me, Mrs. Mortimer." A stout, broad-featured woman with an ample figure and a polka-dot housedress tentatively peered inside. One look at the children standing behind her tenant and she clapped her hands together with a joyous boom. "Ah, so you're back with the wee ones! Mr. Gentry across the hall thought as much."

"I don't know how they manage to keep tabs on me all the time," Tessa muttered to Steven.

He merely smiled. Who could resist watching Tessa?

Nicky tugged at the waistband of Tessa's jeans. "Are we the wee ones?"

The landlady reared slightly. "Most certainly. And you're celebrities, too, making the newspaper the way you did. And here is the lucky groom, I imagine. A shame you weren't in the store when all the fuss was made. You could've been in the picture, too.''

Steven cast his children a dubious sidelong glance. This woman was a character ripe for the picking. What storybook would they drop her into?

Mrs. Mortimer stepped forward to give his hand a solid pump. ''I was so surprised to learn that our Tessa has a gentleman of her own.''

Steven was impressed by the landlady. She appeared to be in her mid-sixties but still moved like a much younger woman. And her mother hen affection for Tessa was as sure as her handshake. If someone was messing about with her girl, she'd make sure he was worthy. The downside was that she was bound to have a lot of questions. Invasive, pesky questions about a relationship that didn't exist. What would his children think of that? He knew he was playing the ultimate hypocrite, weaving a tale for the public, when all the while he was trying to force reality on them. Being a good parent had to be the toughest, most complicated job on earth!

The dilemma solved itself when Natalie and Nicky started moving back down the hallway. He automatically asked them what they were doing.

''We're busy in Tessa's room,'' Natalie replied. ''Looking for her dowry.''

Tessa nodded, realizing their absence was best. ''Go ahead, then.''

''Isn't that touchin','' Mrs. Mortimer purred before snapping her chin up to the adults. ''Now then, you two, where did you first meet? You have to give me the scoop, so I can pass it round the building.''

"New York City," Tessa replied. "Last year actually, while I was still based in Paris."

Paris? She'd lived in Paris? Steven found himself on edge, hungry for more details. A stupid move, since it would only make her all the more real, all the more irresistible.

Mrs. Mortimer sighed. "A romantic place, that New York City."

Steven tried to turn the tables on her. "So, have you ever been to New York, Mrs. Mortimer?"

"No, but I've seen *Breakfast at Tiffany's* dozens of times. A girl could have quite an adventure waltzing round Fifth Avenue." She closed her eyes with a wistful sound, as though temporarily stepping into Audrey Hepburn's shoes. She was back all too soon, however, encouraging Tessa to go on.

"Well, Steven lives in New York. We happened to meet in Central Park. It was a windy day, and . . . my scarf blew off. He chased it down. We shared my picnic lunch. . . ."

Steven picked up the story, curving a hand around her waist. "It was perfect. Spontaneous combustion between two lonely people."

Tessa's eyes widened at the catch in his voice, then at the huge palm that was kneading into the small of her back. There wasn't much to her clingy knit top and he suddenly hit upon bare skin just above her belt. He quickly dropped his hand, but it was too late. She felt as though he'd branded her with a hot iron.

Tessa worked to keep her tone and expression placid. "Anyway, he thought he'd surprise me with a proposal. When he arrived here and found out about the contest, he thought he'd take a chance at an even bigger surprise."

Mrs. Mortimer clasped her hands beneath her fleshy chin. "Isn't it just like in the movies? A real stroke of fate."

The children reappeared then. Steven's parental instincts brought the fine hairs on his neck to life. They'd probably had an in-depth discussion about the landlady and were closing in on her for the kill.

Nicky stepped up boldly, his face alive with curiosity. "Is this your house?"

Mrs. Mortimer was surprised by the question. "Why, yes. It has been for thirty years."

"Can Tessa leave here anytime she wants?"

"Leave?" Mrs. Mortimer's thick gray brows drew down in confusion. "Certainly."

"You got a big oven?" Natalie asked as Nicky tugged on her sleeve.

Tessa cleared her throat, slanting Natalie a warning frown.

"Oh, yeah." Natalie turned to Nicky. "Mrs. Mortimer is a real-life lady. I'm sure she cooks only good things in her oven."

The landlady pinkened with pleasure. "I'm baking peach pies today. Which reminds me, I came up to invite you to have a slice."

"I usually help Mrs. Mortimer test her pies," Tessa told the children. "But I don't think she'd mind if you took my place this time."

"Can we, Daddy?" Natalie asked, clasping her hands together.

Steven paused. He didn't really want to let go of the only thing standing between him and Tessa's seduction attempt. But how could he say no to those twin sets of longing eyes? "Go on, enjoy yourselves."

Mrs. Mortimer led them out, saying they'd be a half hour or so.

Steven shook his head in wonder as the door closed again. "For a minute there, I thought your landlady was going to be cast as the witch in Hansel and Gretel. But a signal from you instantly changed Natalie's direction. How'd you do that?"

"Well, we girls have a few secrets between us."

"You are nothing short of magical!"

Tessa's mouth curved enticingly. "A rub to my back always brings out the genie in me."

"Yeah, sorry about that." Steven instinctively shoved his hands in the pockets of his slacks. "I was just trying to help you embellish our story."

"Yes, it was just the right touch."

Exactly his thought. Her skin was like smooth, warm satin beneath his fingertips.

"Now, what were you saying about spontaneous combustion between two lonely people...." She moved in on him again, fire in her green eyes.

This was his fault. He had sounded as if he meant those words. And maybe he did. But to act on his desires wouldn't be right. "I wouldn't mind a taste of that ale I spotted in your cupboard," he quickly said. "If it's not too much trouble."

She rolled her eyes. "All right. C'mon, then."

He set two tall glasses on the table while she stood at the counter to unscrew the cap on the large bottle. She turned and began to pour. "I'll be Mother."

"Like you've been doing all day."

His husky voice made her heart trip. "You know what I mean. It's a figure of speech over here."

He took a long draw of the amber liquid. "I know. It's my clever way of thanking you for opening up your life to my kids."

"Oh." She set the bottle down on the table between them with a thump, tiring of his efforts to hem her in as a mother figure. "You're very welcome."

He clinked her glass in a toast. "You did everything right."

"Oh, stop!"

"I mean it." Steven sank into a chair, as though burdened by the admission. "It's clear that they have a major crush on you."

"Crushes aren't just for children, you know."

Steven stiffened with awareness as she hovered over him. Bracing her hands on his shoulders, she rested her knee on his thigh. His body felt rock solid, and she began to explore the planes of his chest with a massaging motion of her hands.

"This is a lousy idea, honey."

"Why?"

His heart began to slam in his rib cage. Could she feel it beneath her fingertips? "Because of our age difference for starters. I'm thirty-seven, and what are you, twenty-five?"

"Almost twenty-six!"

He gave her fingers a gentle squeeze, lifting them from the sensitive hollow of his throat.

"The age thing isn't enough of an excuse!"

"It's the whole setup, Tessa. We're only going to be here a few days. I'm sure you're not in the habit of having brief affairs."

"I might be!"

"I figure you've never tried it, so you don't know for sure, right?"

"Why do you say that?"

"There is something so fresh and honest about the way you approach me. It's a dead giveaway."

Tessa nudged her knee deeper into his thigh muscles. "Don't tell me that you haven't imagined us together. I know you have... and so have I."

He compressed his lips. She was dangerous, drawing him into the kind of intimacy shared by lovers. It worried him that she just might have the power to unearth passions and secrets best kept buried. "I don't want to pursue this," he said firmly. When she looked hurt, he added, "In so many ways I'm drawn to you—"

"Well then!"

"But I'm not going to take advantage of the artificial circumstances we've found ourselves in and knowingly start something that will be over before it's barely begun. There are too many emotions at stake here—including mine."

Her mouth curved saucily. "I'm going to kiss you now, I think."

"How refreshingly naive of you to tell me."

She cupped his jawline in her hands and sank down to straddle his hips. "You are a blighter," she said with husky conviction. "Our attraction must be just sexual, after all."

Despite all his fine intentions, he instinctively opened his mouth to hers, welcoming the pressure of her lips, the invasive smoothness of her tongue. She shifted on his lap, crushing her breasts against his chest. Liquid lightning raced through his veins, heating him, dazing him. He could do unforgettable things to her. But it would be wrong, knowing that it would fill her with false hopes.

Bracing his hands against her shoulders, he eventually pushed her up.

"Can't you just relax and enjoy it?" she softly asked, disappointed.

He shook his head.

Tessa could feel her face flaming up and the compelling urge to justify her advances. "Okay, it's true that I take my relationships very seriously. But there is something meaningful happening between us. Can't you see that all the admissions you've made during the past two days are every bit as intimate as sex itself?"

The observation disconcerted him because it was probably true. "I guess I've been talking way too much!"

"So, ask yourself why. Why a guarded man afraid of marriage would open up to a woman he barely knows!" She glared down at him. "If it's easier, ask yourself why I'd bother to seduce a guarded old sod like you, with all your family baggage! Something big is happening here!"

"Can't you see I'm thinking of you, too?"

Tessa lifted her chin petulantly. "No. I believe you find me inconvenient, now that I've served my purpose."

"Oh, Tessa!"

She made a rush for the front door and flung it open.

"Are you kicking me out!"

"For the children's sake, I won't. But I can't stand to be alone with a bastard like you another minute. We're going downstairs to have some peach pie, and pretend we're having a perfectly marvelous time, and then I'm going to say goodbye—forever!"

"OH, MOTHER." Steven looked up from the paper-work before him on the sitting room desk. "You're finally back."

Millicent secured the door, then eased out of her black all-weather coat. "It's not that late yet. Barely midnight."

Steven couldn't help but think of all the evenings she'd hustled herself and the children into pajamas. "Seems late for you."

Her face pinkened to the rich shade of her chiffon cocktail dress. "Is it? I was having such a wonderful time I barely noticed."

His eyes crinkled in approval. No one deserved time for herself more than she did. "Tell me all about it."

She set her purse on the coffee table and sank onto the settee. "You're still working. I won't bother you now."

Steven set his pencil aside, stood up and stretched. Millicent was easing off her silver open-toed shoes, making an attempt to appear blasé. But she was ob-viously more excited than he'd seen her in a long while. It was ironic that she would happen to fly so high on a day when he'd tumbled so low. "C'mon now, I really want to hear about your evening. And besides, I feel it's my duty. You're ready to burst and it might be dangerous for your blood pressure." He sat beside her, took her feet in his lap and gently rubbed them.

She drew in a deep breath, obviously eager for the confidence. "I had a marvelous evening. Old friends, flashy, uncomfortable shoes and a binding girdle that I plan to take off very soon."

"So who made up the wild bunch?"

Millicent's keen eyes narrowed. "I know you're teasing, but we can still stir up a little action when we try. Anyway, it was ladies' night, four of us in all. Countess Elise Van Tileckie, Agnes Filborn and Dame Judith Westcott."

Steven looked lost. "Can't say I know any of them."

"You've never been one to keep up with my friends. I imagine you don't even remember my ties to the DeWildes."

He gently kneaded her arches, frowning. "I really don't. What *is* your connection with them?"

"My good friend Celeste is from the Montiefiori side of the family," she told him. "A charming woman."

"Isn't she the one who abandoned her family?"

"Yes, I'm afraid so. But it's my understanding that her grandchildren have turned out very well. Very well."

"I'm not interested in making any social connections this trip. Please don't set anything up for me." He stared down at her sternly. "Promise me you won't."

She solemnly raised a slender hand. "I promise I won't introduce you to another soul unless you ask me to."

He sighed with relief. "Now, tell me about your night."

She snuggled into the cushions. "Well, we started off with *Sunset Boulevard* at the Adelphi, then it was on to dinner at Wiltons. You know how I love that place. It's the absolute best for a typical English meal. We started off with beluga caviar—and before you scold me about my low-salt diet, I must say I only had a taste. Then for the main course I had their delicious lamb chops. And then I had the most tasty dessert—"

Steven beat her to the finish. "Wiltons' sherry trifle."

Millicent laughed. "Am I that predictable?"

"Not often enough, unfortunately."

She gasped in feigned dismay. "You never stop!"

Steven couldn't believe Millicent's transformation since breakfast. Her dancing eyes and merry tone took a decade off her age. The image both pleased and troubled him. He was happy to see her out on the town again, but at the same time he was clearly reminded that he and the children were holding her back from the life she loved so well.

"What's the matter, dear? You look troubled."

"Oh, I was just thinking how you've been so limited lately to brief outings in Manhattan. It feels good to see you this excited, in your element, in a favorite city with your pals."

"It is wonderful," she confided, much to her own surprise. "I originally made many of these friends on business trips with your dad, as you know, when making the right connections and schmoozing were so much a part of our business. It was enjoyable, don't get me wrong. But now all the pressure's off. It's one of the few advantages to getting older, but a big one. Now everyone's more relaxed and focused mainly on socializing and enjoying their grandchildren."

"But not many of them are caring for their grandchildren like you are."

"So that's what's on your mind!" She swung her legs off his lap and patted his hand. "I am happy with my choice. Those two monkeys are treasures to me."

"I'm sure they made a good showing round the old dinner table tonight."

Millicent smiled as she reached up to remove her diamond earrings. "You bet your life they did! It's the only competitive bone left in this old body of mine."

"Maybe, if you think things over from a fresh viewpoint, you'll see that my nanny idea is a good one."

"Hah!"

"You'd have the freedom to take off whenever you pleased."

Her defenses began to rise, deepening the lines in her face. "I'm satisfied with our arrangement as it is. And it'll stay as it is until you find a better alternative...or I die," she added dramatically. "But I warn you, I'll refuse to die until you get on track. You can either get hitched or quit your grumbling—or try both in a perfect world. Speaking of perfection, how did things go with Tessa today?"

"Fine. She got to Natalie somehow and convinced her that a real live friend was worth more than a fantasy one."

"Very clever, seeing that Natalie has so much control over Nicky. You have to give Tessa a lot of credit."

"When Tessa makes up her mind about something, she follows through."

Millicent turned her sunburst earrings over in her hand with a thoughtful frown. "There's a finality to your tone that I don't like."

Damn if she didn't always pick up on his thoughts! "Please don't analyze my tone, not at this hour."

His sharp request made her all the more suspicious. "Something went wrong, I can tell."

He sat up straighter, traces of pride in his affront. "She happened to like me. She tried to kiss me."

"Oh, really? Did she succeed?"

He studied his hands, forcing his fingers to remain limp when he wanted to curl them into angry fists. "Well, yeah."

"Did you like it?"

"Very much."

"So you offended her in retaliation!"

"She was the one to decide we should never see each other again."

"A technicality, I bet. A last-ditch effort to save her pride."

"You had to be there to understand."

"Not at all. No one knows you better than your mother." She rose to her feet with a sigh. "Let's turn in. We can look at this better in the light of day."

"Oh, I can't. I have to go out for a while."

She pivoted on her stockinged feet with surprise. "Why?"

He wasn't about to concern her with the trials of his uncertain business deal with Butler Toys. Millicent could handle the drama of his love life, but business was a far harsher reality to her. Steven had promised his father on his deathbed that Millicent would never be troubled again with any business worries. Franklin Butler's refusal to seal the deal on the Galaxy Ranger rights more than qualified as one large worry. Steven had just gotten off the phone with Barry Lambert, who was patiently waiting at his Chelsea flat with a gallon of coffee and sharpened pencils.

They intended to spend the night looking for a certain magic that would give his Rangers new appeal.

Tension crackled in the silence. Millicent couldn't resist having her say. "You're meeting that Barry Lambert again, aren't you. London's pied piper to the city's bimbos."

Steven inhaled sharply, realizing her colorful conclusion-jumping was a godsend for once. "Yes, Mother, I am going over to Barry's notorious den of delights. If you need me for anything, his number is in my address book near the phone."

"Are you sure your precious children are tucked in for the night?"

He blinked wearily. "Yes. We've been through glasses of water, a guessing game and an emergency nail clipping of Nicky's big toes."

"You can't be too careful in a strange hotel room." Pink chiffon swirled round her slim hips as she zoomed toward the closed bedroom door.

Steven returned to the desk to collect his notes, hoping to ease them into the pockets of his jacket while she was preoccupied. He made quick work of it, folding the papers into squares and stuffing them in all the slash openings.

Meanwhile, Millicent eased open the bedroom door, her stance immediately softening as she slipped into the quiet cocoon. A pale stream of light flowed in, as well, allowing her to make out the two tiny forms lost in the queen-size bed beside the one she occupied herself. She was disgruntled that Steven hadn't followed on her heels, full of apology. Finding the bedcovers loose, most likely from some sort of tussle, she went through the motherly ritual of tucking in the ends, first on Nicky's side, then on Natalie's.

Natalie was lying on her side facing her brother, a Galaxy Ranger nestled in the curve of her arm. Though she liked softer, more feminine dolls, she was her daddy's girl through and through, always hoping to please him with her interest in the company.

Millicent didn't have many rules, but she did have one about sleeping with Rangers. They were made of hard plastic, all wrong for cuddling. Ever so gently she pried the figure loose. Natalie made a whiny sound in her sleep and rolled flat on her back, her tide of brown hair spilling across the pillow.

The movement caused Millicent to gasp. There, in all its glistening glory, was the Montiefiori pearl choker, fastened around the child's throat!

CHAPTER EIGHT

MILLICENT CLUTCHED HER THROAT as she stared down at the pearls around her granddaughter's neck, her heart tripping like a mallet against her chest. She could only speculate as to the worth of Celeste's necklace. *Priceless—priceless—priceless* kept flashing before her eyes like a neon sign.

So how did it end up here? On little Natalie, of all people? Surely Steven had no idea. Did he? Her mind whirling with threats of grand larceny, the fraud squad and wailing sirens, Millicent sought a reasonable explanation. Unfortunately, even her fertile imagination couldn't manage to come up with anything that would throw an innocent light on her granddaughter. For some reason Natalie had taken a liking to the necklace and most likely smuggled it out of Tessa's flat in her purse.

Millicent hovered over the bed, trembling nervously. How awful if she had been caught redhanded! Hadn't Steven paid a bit of attention to the children at that woman's flat? Though she hated doing it, Millicent couldn't help but crown her son the dumbbell of the day. He was so busy denying his attraction to Tessa that he'd completely missed the caper of the century!

Millicent jumped a little when she realized a shadow was blocking the light from the sitting room.

"Everything okay, Mother?" Steven whispered from the doorway.

"Yes, dear, yes." She scrambled to tuck the sheet up to Natalie's chin for the time being. "If you're going, you may as well go."

"Don't you want to nail me with one last 'Shame on you, rogue son'?"

Millicent hurried to join him, pushing him back over the threshold, safely out of pearl-viewing range. "I'm too tired to bicker tonight."

He hovered over her for a pensive moment, then kissed her forehead. "Good night, then."

"Steven?"

He paused in midstep with a knowing look. "Yes?"

She turned her huge diamond solitaire on her finger. "Did Tessa give the children anything?"

"Aside from her time and lunch, no. Why?"

"Nothing. I just wanted to make sure you appreciated what she did for you."

He took some time to analyze her motives. "Oh, I get it!"

"You do?"

"You went into the bedroom, tucked them in—"

"So you did see—"

"Yes! While I was working I could hear them bouncing around, tearing up the bedding, but I just shouted at them to settle down. I'm sure a mother— like Tessa—would've taken the time to go in there and calm things down and put the room back in order. Now, as handy as that would be, it's not reason enough to marry. Okay?"

All she could think of was how madly his brain was ticking at such a late hour. For a party boy he was certainly agitated. "How angry was she when you parted ways?"

"Very."

"Oh, dear. So she's fresh out of goodwill for all of us, I suppose."

Steven bit his lip, summoning his last ounce of patience. One second she was shooing him off, the next she had him under the bright lights for another round of questions. "If you're worried that the children noticed a problem when we left Tessa's, don't be. Everyone parted on friendly terms."

"What did our chatterbox Natalie have to say about the time you all spent with Tessa?"

"Come to think of it, she was especially quiet during the taxi ride home. She seemed quite satisfied with the day's events, though."

She had a right to be! "Did she say anything at all, Steven?"

"No. But if there'd been something big on her mind, she would have confided in me. She always does."

Millicent rolled her eyes. It seemed her son was a fool for women of all sizes! Perhaps he was the one who needed the guiding hand of a nanny. "You may as well go, Steven," she said briskly with a shooing motion.

Steven reached for his jacket, taking care that the paper in the pockets wouldn't crackle and give away his real mission. "If you're pouting because your matchmaking scheme didn't work, I advise you to drop it. Tessa's made it plain that she's through with us, and that's final."

Millicent secured the door behind her son with a sigh of relief. It was best to have him out of the way.

He'd already flubbed his relationship with the Montiefiori granddaughter, and another misstep could land him behind bars!

She returned to the bedroom, gently turning Natalie on her side to unclasp the necklace. The pearls, warmed by the girl's skin, fell into her hands without mishap. She tiptoed back out, still fuming about her son. Steven had a nerve implying that she was growing lax in her duties by looking for a nanny. Luckily for him, she was the one who had nurtured the Sanderses' social connections and she was the one who possessed enough tact to get them out of this mess. An immediate call to Tessa seemed wise, along with the soothing reassurance that the pearls were in the best of care. Now, where were her reading glasses...?

She found the spectacles on the television, then sat down at the desk, spreading the necklace out before her. "Let's hope Steven didn't commit Tessa's number to memory...." She opened his address book, flipping through the pages full of his scrawl. She was nearly at wit's end when she realized that she was looking under *M* for Montiefiori rather than *J* for Jones. She turned back several pages to find Tessa's name printed in bold, black strokes, along with her address on White's Row and her telephone number.

Adjusting her lenses at the correct angle on her nose, she lifted the receiver and carefully punched in the proper numbers. After all, it was nearly 1:00 a.m., and calling at this hour was an inconvenience. The phone rang a few times, then there was a click, and Tessa's sweet voice, thick with sleep, came on the line.

"Hello, Tessa. This is— Oh, you recognized my voice? How clever of you." Millicent went on to explain what had happened. Tessa suggested coming straight over, but Millicent suggested she wait till morning. The children were asleep, after all, and the choker would be extremely safe with her.

With a sigh of gratitude, she replaced the receiver in its cradle. Thank heavens the girl hadn't sounded suspicious. Shocked? Yes. Annoyed? A little. But Millicent sensed Tessa trusted her at her word and would send up no alarm.

By the time Millicent was drifting off to sleep, her priorities had seesawed back to romance. Steven was out of prison blues and back in a tuxedo, standing in the receiving line at a wedding reception rather than in a chain gang.

TESSA ARRIVED at the London Hilton promptly at six o'clock on Sunday morning. Her urgent knock was answered by Millicent, who was dressed for the day in a jade sweater and black slacks. Tessa hadn't taken as much care with her appearance. After several hours of tossing and turning, she'd pulled on some old jeans and a wraparound jacket of her own design, made of scraps of her old clothing along the lines of a memory quilt. A tug of a hairbrush, a lunge for her purse, and off she'd gone.

"Thanks for waiting until morning," Millicent said, ushering her inside. If she thought Tessa's outfit was uncommon, or dead common, she didn't show it. All Tessa saw was a blend of gratitude and terror in her regal face.

"It was difficult to wait. But I understand about the children."

"Yes, they need a good talking to and it would've been futile in the middle of the night."

Millicent gestured to a comfortable chair at the small circular table near the window. "I hope my call didn't upset you too much."

Tessa's denial was wan. Of course it had! All kinds of possible disasters had raced through her mind as she groped for her bedside lamp and telephone. It might have been a relative in a car crash. Or a reporter unmasking her fake engagement.

It might have been Steven, full of apologies that would erase the embarrassment she was suffering. Tessa cringed now, as she did every time she reviewed her failed attempt at seduction. What had been a sincere attempt on her part to indulge in some mutual pleasure had been twisted by him into a May-December fiasco. He'd deliberately reduced her to some kind of desperate Lolita!

Instead, it was Millicent's smoky voice on the wire, so distressed that even the wary Tessa couldn't mistake her sincerity. Then, of course, she'd dropped the bombshell that Natalie had absconded with her precious pearls. The whole thing was incredible, including the fact that Millicent had been so certain of their authenticity.

"As you can see, I've ordered up tea," Millicent announced, clearly trying to please her. Too bad Steven hadn't picked up any of her social skills.

Tessa graciously took in the delectable-looking assortment of pastries arranged on a huge silver tray. She was starving. But she couldn't touch a bite until she had her necklace back. She reached into her roomy shoulder bag for the blue DeWilde's box. "If you don't mind, Millicent, I'd like to put the pearls where they belong right off. Since they do belong to my employers and all."

"Of course. How thoughtless of me." Millicent moved to the desk, where her jewelry box sat out in the open, already unlocked.

"I was to return them to Gabriel DeWilde this evening," Tessa felt compelled to explain.

"He must have amazing trust in you to leave them in your care."

She reddened. It did sound unbelievable. And Millicent did seem way too interested. Tessa couldn't decide if Millicent was being guileful or remarkably nosy. In the past she'd proven to be a blend of both!

"As I explained on the phone, I took charge of the necklace the moment I found it, putting it in here with my pieces. It's been locked in the room safe until now."

Tessa joined her at the desk, setting her small blue box beside the bigger brown one. She clearly saw fresh emotion shimmer in the older woman's gray eyes as she gazed down at the puffed satin lining bearing the DeWilde name in gold lettering. Millicent's hands shook slightly as she removed her own white velvet sheath from the necklace and transferred it to the DeWilde box. Tessa couldn't help wondering where Steven had been through all the drama. Whose bed he'd warmed instead of hers.

"He isn't back yet," Millicent gently said in reply to Tessa's wandering glance.

"Yet?"

"He's been out for hours, at the flat of a business associate."

"Oh, of course. None of my affair, really."

"It's obvious that you care, and I am telling you the truth," Millicent assured her.

Tessa looked sheepish. "It seems my image as a cool woman of the nineties needs some work."

"Not as far as I'm concerned, it doesn't. There's nothing more attractive than a modern woman going after what she wants most. Come, let's sit and enjoy our breakfast."

Tessa laughed as she slipped her case back in her purse. "Yes, let's. I know better than to ever try to get round you!"

Millicent measured her with unabashed delight, taking the remark as the ultimate compliment. "You are so ideal in every way that I'm sure I must be dreaming!"

Tessa held a chair out for Millicent and poured their tea into the hotel's lovely china teacups.

"Thanks for playing 'mother,' dear."

Tessa's mouth thinned ruefully. "That's what your son said to me yesterday."

"Did he?" Millicent regarded her in astonishment. "I'm sure he was referring to your handling of the children in that compliment."

"I'm sure he was," she agreed dryly. "He's worked very hard to keep their needs our only focus."

"Steven's really quite wonderful, but sometimes he's too intense over the children's welfare. Clearing up this misunderstanding I've caused has made him jumpier than usual. Among other things, I imagine."

Tessa thought she saw a flicker of mischief in the older woman's eyes. She raised the creamer between them.

"None for me, dear. I'm on a regulated diet, which I already grievously broke last night while out on the town."

Tessa tonged a sugar cube and dropped it into her cup. "Have you many friends in London, then?"

Millicent made a lavish gesture, her ego inflating. "Why, yes. All kinds of them."

"You must have spent a lot of time here over the years."

Millicent slid her teacup onto her saucer in a thoughtful motion. "Intermittently, when it didn't interfere with my raising Steven. My late husband Robert and I had such fun traveling all over the world, promoting Sanders Novelties. As with any business, half the battle is making the right connections. It's my philosophy that having a good set of contacts—what is called 'networking' these days—makes life a lot simpler and more satisfying."

Tessa made a show of stirring her tea as she attempted to piece together the facts she'd collected and compare them to her suspicions. There was every possibility that at some point in her travels this society matron had crossed paths with the DeWilde-Montiefiori clan. And the better Tessa got to know Millicent, the more out of character her daft behavior at the store seemed. Gabe had called her moves to win the contest diabolically clever, and Tessa had to agree they were. But her motives might prove to be quite simple.

It seemed very likely that Millicent knew she was a Montiefiori and was making a wild attempt to link her family with Tessa's. A networking system extraordinaire! Millicent had no reason to consider a perfect stranger modeling a wedding dress to be a worthy match for her son, but the granddaughter of one of her contemporaries would hold an undeniable appeal. And an acquaintanceship with Tessa's family explained why she had known the pearls were of great value. Yes, it appeared that Millicent was trying to make an archaic sort of society match for her son.

Determined to get to the bottom of things, Tessa steered the conversation in the right direction on a wave of flattery. "I find you amazing, you know."

Millicent beamed. "Why?"

"Because you were observant enough to realize the choker was valuable, for starters."

Millicent's eyes clouded over her teacup and she stiffened slightly. "Plenty of experience with jewelry."

"It occurred to me that you might have seen it before."

Millicent was silent as she considered Tessa's words. "Well, I may have seen it. Everyone I know drips with the good stuff."

The air seemed to hum with tension all of a sudden. Tessa sensed she was probing in the proper place. "You must have wondered why I was entrusted with it, didn't you?"

"Well . . ." Millicent trailed off, again having trouble with what should have been a simple question. "*I'd* have lent it to you for such an important promotion."

"But I still have it, don't I?"

"It seems you do."

Tessa rested her elbows on the table, her gaze keen. "What do you make of that?"

Millicent bit into a scone with a purr. "Have something to eat, Tessa. You remind me of a wayward elf, with that tiny figure."

"Don't try to slide out of this one, Millicent. You might as well tell me the truth."

Millicent huffed in exasperation and set her cup in its saucer with a clink. "All right! I know full well that you're Celeste's granddaughter. Celeste and I were great friends long ago when you were a child. But don't be cross with me. I've been playing your game and have kept the secret from Steven! But why the charade?"

Tessa sat back with a laugh. "I'm simply trying to sell my designs on merit rather than family pull. I have every intention of revealing my identity as soon as I'm established."

Millicent clapped her hands together with delight. "Just as I thought! What a wonderful stunt. Best of luck!"

Tessa never ceased to be amazed by Millicent's seeming inability to grasp the consequences of her interference. "Wait a minute now, Millicent. You're a little more than a cheerleader here. You've put my promotion scheme in real jeopardy by making it appear that I'm to be married myself!"

Millicent showed absolutely no remorse. "Marriage is fun, dear," she said, her expression softening. "You'll like it."

Tessa gaped at her, struggling for words. "Your son has no wish to get married, and neither do I."

"If you look me straight in the eye and tell me you're not interested in Steven, I'll escort you to the door and never bother you again."

"But I don't wish to marry!"

"That's not what I said."

"Your son is not interested in me."

Millicent's eyes narrowed. "That's a damn lie and we both know it."

"Well, his mating rituals are the strangest I've ever seen, then. I've thrown myself at him and he won't—take me!" She pressed her hands to her eyes. "Bloody embarrassing, that."

"To the contrary, girl. It's hopeful." Millicent reached out to give her hands a squeeze. "Very hopeful."

Tessa blinked in confusion. "I don't get it."

"Steven is afraid to give himself up to love again. He's had his share of casual relationships and breezed through them with barely a ripple of response." Millicent shook Tessa's hands fiercely. "Don't you see? You're the first one to really rock his boat. For him to turn you down, when he's so obviously interested, is a wonderful sign! He's simply frightened of falling for you. He knows that this physical tumble will be one he can't easily turn away from."

"What's put him off starting over?" Tessa found the nerve to ask.

"You know about Renee dying so unexpectedly."

"Yes, that must have been awful for all of you."

"It was especially tragic for Steven. We all knew of her bout with rheumatic fever as a child, but the extent of the damage was not known."

Tessa frowned in confusion. "I don't follow, Millicent."

"The, uh, attack happened in bed. Steven returned home from a business trip one night—"

"And couldn't awaken her?"

Millicent cleared her throat and dabbed a napkin to her lips. "No, dear. She wasn't asleep when it happened."

"Oh!" Tessa's eyes grew wide. "They were . . ."

Millicent allowed the implication to stand on its own. "I'm telling you this only because I think you really care for him and should understand why he shuts down in the face of emotional risk."

Tessa absorbed the implications of the situation. Steven probably thought that his lovemaking had killed his wife. No wonder he didn't care to get close to another woman. What an awful burden to carry!

"Passions can run so strong after separations. Steven did his fair share of traveling, like his father, and it can make for a roller coaster kind of existence, gone one week, home the next. Unlike me, Renee wasn't interested in any of Steven's business affairs and preferred her clubs and shopping to travel. In any case, this last reunion put too much of a strain on Renee's heart. It gave out and she was gone, right then and there. Steven's never confided his deepest feelings to me, but one can imagine what it must have been like to have someone you loved die in your arms that way. The guilt and anger and memories would change the way one viewed sex forever."

"I guess I've been pretty hard on him."

"Believe me, he does it to himself. And it's a mistake! Renee did foolish things that put her in peril all along, like smoking cigarettes." She broke off in exasperation. "It's no use me arguing with him because he's dropped a curtain on the past. He won't have me speaking of it at all."

Tessa nibbled on a bun, avoiding her gaze. "I appreciate the insight, Millicent, but I don't think it's going to change things between us."

"It already has. You're not nearly as angry with him."

"Well, I am partly to blame for our problems, for coming on too strong. I couldn't have handled a brief fling and he knew it. Damn, I hate that he's been so right about me!"

"Well, don't mistake him for Einstein. He didn't even notice Natalie had your pearls!" Their laughter mingled for a moment, lightening the mood. "It's up to you, but I can tell you how to reach him."

Tessa shrugged. "I don't know, Millicent."

"It's nothing drastic. Just let him know you aren't trying to pressure him or change him. Those are the qualities he dislikes in me. And confess to him who you really are before he reads about that in the papers, too."

"A surefire formula?"

"Nothing's ever certain in this world, but it's your best chance. He's built a protective wall around himself since Renee's passing."

"How he must have loved her."

Millicent grew wistful. "Yes, indeed. But look at the bright side. It proves he has a capacity to love unreservedly. You just think about it all, dear."

"All right." Tessa freshened their tea. "On the condition that you tell me all about your antics with my grandmother. I was as close to her as she'd allow anyone in the family to be and I would cherish any stories you have."

By the time the pair emptied the teapot, the children were moving around in the bedroom. Natalie startled them when she raced through the doorway with her hands on her throat.

"Grandma! Grandma! I've been robbed!"

"No, poppet, *I've* been robbed."

The sound of Tessa's voice shocked the young girl and she stumbled to a halt just short of the round table. She humbly lowered her eyes and dropped her chin to rest on her flannel nightie. "Hi, Tessa."

"Hallo, hallo, busy one."

"I discovered the necklace on you last night and called Tessa," Millicent said with a measure of sternness that seemed unnatural to her.

Natalie stomped her foot and gave a surprised cry. "You're a tattletale, Grandma. And you tell me not to be one."

"Well, there's a difference between reporting Nicky's juice spills to me and my reporting an important theft to Tessa."

"A smart girl like Natalie knows that." Tessa crooked her finger, summoning her closer. Natalie shuffled her bare feet through the carpet, her head still lowered. Tessa scooped her onto her lap and gently stroked her hair. "Would you mind telling me exactly why you took those pearls?"

"Because you need a dowry. To give to Daddy!"

"Dowries aren't expected much anymore."

"But I thought I was helping. And I wanted to pretend I was you. It really worked, too. I wore the necklace to bed and dreamed of being a beautiful bride who sews dresses for a big fancy store."

Tessa warmed under the child's adoring eyes. "I think you should start smaller," she advised. "Maybe doll clothes."

"I imagine Tessa made the jacket she's wearing," Millicent said.

Natalie traced her finger over some of the quilted squares on the jacket's sleeve. "It's very pretty."

"Each piece is cut from an old garment of mine. Each has a wonderful memory or two attached to it. When you get older, you can make one yourself."

"Let's do it now!"

Tessa met Millicent's twinkling eyes over the table. "You'll need time to collect the clothes and the memories. But I'm sure if you're really interested in sewing, your grandmother can arrange lessons."

Millicent reached over and tapped her grand-daughter's shoulder. "Before we go too far afield, Natalie, I think you owe Tessa an apology for taking her pearls."

Natalie sniffed and straightened her spine. "I only borrowed them."

"But taking things is wrong, no matter what."

"Even if I'm starving for food, Grandma?"

"Poppet . . ." Tessa warned.

"Okay. I know it was wrong. I'm sorry. Will you still be my friend?"

"We're the best of friends. No matter what."

Natalie cautiously looked around the suite. "Does Daddy know what I did?"

Tessa looked to Millicent for that answer.

Millicent shook her head. "Not yet he doesn't. And it certainly won't help his nerves any."

Natalie stroked Tessa's cheek with her slender hand. "We don't want to wreck Daddy's nerves, do we?" she asked, her voice cajoling.

Tessa smiled, thinking that there were better ways to do that. "As far as I'm concerned, this matter is forgotten."

"You promise?"

"Promises are very important to children, Tessa," Millicent hastily cautioned. "Parents learn to make them conservatively, knowing it's only right to keep them."

"Yes, of course. I do promise, however. No harm's been done and you've politely apologized."

"Oh, thanks." With a squeal, Natalie wound her arms around Tessa's neck, burrowing in her lush blond hair. Within seconds, Tessa felt another pair of hands on her thigh. She peered over Natalie's shoulder to find her little brother dressed only in his underpants.

Millicent was appalled. "Nicholas Steven Sanders! Where are your pajamas?"

He rubbed his rounded tummy. "I lost 'em."

Millicent rose with an exasperated sigh, captured his hand and guided him in the direction of the bedroom. "Can you just imagine some poor nanny trying to keep up with these stunts? Thievery? Nudity?"

The little boy trailed after her, shaking his head. "I can't imagine."

Tessa and Natalie looked at each other and began to laugh.

"It's a good thing we got you now, Tessa. Grandma gets really tired sometimes."

Tessa ruffled her hair in loving exasperation. "Oh, Natalie." She knew that what the little girl said was the truth, though, just by looking at Millicent. Undoubtedly she'd lost a lot of sleep last night alone. Up until midnight, only to discover the pearls. It must have been a wild night for the children's grandmother.

"Will you stay and play?" Natalie asked. "Then Grandma can take a nap."

Images of Steven appearing with an empty champagne bottle under his arm made her hesitate. Despite Millicent's attempt to whitewash his absence, Tessa was certain he'd brushed off her advances yesterday only to search out a better offer. But Natalie's hungry eyes overruled all her more petty thoughts. She couldn't believe how easily these children were able to wrap her up in knots!

"I suppose we could sew something," Tessa suggested with inspiration. "I have a chest of supplies in the boot of my car."

"Can we make some little doll dresses, like the ones at the museum?"

Tessa rolled her eyes. She'd been thinking along the lines of a hand-stitched potholder. But she knew she'd brought this on herself. Natalie wanted to be like her, and she'd admitted to starting her sewing career with doll clothes. "I suppose we could put together something simple. Have you a favorite baby doll?"

"Daddy's got all the dolls we need."

"What?"

"You'll see." Natalie bounced off her lap and set off at a run. "Nicky, Nicky, guess what?"

Tessa popped to her feet and called after her, "But it'll be a very small project. I can't stay all day. Really! I can't! I'm dining at the Savoy tonight. Do you hear?"

CHAPTER NINE

"I THINK YOU'VE JUST brought me along for protection."

Steven turned a deaf ear to Barry Lambert's tauntings as he hustled him into the Hilton's empty elevator later that afternoon. They were a pair of misfits, Steven in casual slacks and brown pullover, topped with his tan jacket, Barry in a sharp black suit with white shirt and tie.

Steven shifted from one foot to the other as they rode up in the elevator, anxious to make the quick changeover to prosperous businessman. A shower and his double-breasted navy wool suit were bound to do the trick. "It's three-thirty now," he said with a glance at his watch. "Franklin Butler's birthday bash begins at five. If we stick together, we just might get back out of here in time for our preparty business meeting with him."

Barry's mouth curved beneath his thin mustache. "You're afraid of your mum."

"Just remember that I don't want her to know there's any glitch in this business deal. Or that we were up all night trying to come up with a way to make the Galaxy Rangers more appealing to your stubborn old boss."

"So you'd rather she think we were out on the town all night."

"Given only those two options, yes. You see, my father refused to move on with the times at one point and nearly lost everything. I managed to save the day, but she still fears that it could happen again. The stress would be more than her old heart could handle."

"She seems very sturdy to me."

"She'd also insist on confronting Franklin Butler and really dig her heels in the way she did when my father was alive."

"Maybe she can come up with an inspired idea."

"No, Barry, she'll simply pressure Butler into unconditional surrender."

"But she blames me for your supposed shenanigans," Barry protested. "Funny that, when you must party a bit back in New York."

"She's always tended to blame my evil companions for trouble, starting way back in grammar school," Steven said fondly. "And she's happily set in her ways."

Barry looked pained. "I should've waited in the car."

"No, no. I want you to keep her occupied while I shower and dress. While you run interference, I can dig for some final-hour inspiration."

Barry brushed some lint off his jacket sleeve. "Let's face it, we've come up empty. Franklin doesn't know why he thinks the Galaxy Ranger collection lacks pizazz and we can't come up with a new angle."

"I'm sure I'm stalled because I think the action figures are fine as they are. They sell well in the States, and deep down I don't care to change them."

"I've worked for Franklin Butler for seven years and I know he likes to put his stamp on everything. If we could somehow spark his imagination, even with a small idea, he'd take the reins and turn the venture into his own."

Steven made a frustrated noise. "Why fix something that's not broken?"

"Curse of the creative mind."

"Curse of the egomaniac!"

Barry shrugged elegantly. "A blend of both, I suppose. But if this expansion is to happen at all, you will have to bend some."

"I know it. And I'm willing. But any changes have to be good ones and not take away from the legends I've already had written up for the Rangers." Steven sagged against the safety rail, closing his eyes for a moment. "I just feel so boxed in by the concept. For me it's already complete. Hell, maybe this deal just isn't meant to be."

"You seem to blame fate for a lot of your shortcomings," Barry mumbled on the tail of a contrived cough as they stopped at the eighth floor.

Steven exited the elevator car and turned. "Did I hear you right?"

Barry shrugged his shoulders, easing through the doors as they began to glide closed. "I just said you seem game for your homecoming."

Steven gave him a nudge. "Yeah, sure."

They tramped down the corridor, Steven in the lead. He had his room key in hand, but to his surprise didn't need it. The doorknob turned as he grasped it. Disturbed by the easy entry, he whisked the door open in a panic. The scene inside was one he had never expected to see again in his lifetime—Tessa

Jones in the company of his children. She was seated on the floor in the center of the sitting room, studiously guiding a needle and thread through a piece of fabric. Natalie was nestled against her side, and Nicky was seated nearby, watching the whole process.

The scene was magic. It all looked so right, so comfortable, so natural that Steven was tempted to climb inside the picture and never come back out again.

But it was too damn risky. Nothing lasted forever. Especially under circumstances like this! Tessa Jones was no nanny with a wish to travel. She was a Londoner with a career that was just starting to go places. It was wrong of her to bond with his children, knowing that their days here were numbered. What was she trying to do to them? To all of them!

Nicky noticed him first and gave a simple wiggle of his chunky fingers.

Irritation, envy and surprise swelled higher in Steven when his son didn't cry out in delight and charge at him like a miniature cyclone. Worse yet, his daughter didn't have the grace to notice him at all! The kids always welcomed him home the moment he arrived.

Even in this innocent setting, Tessa looked wild and provocative, her hair loose and her features unguarded. Her come-on yesterday had left him aching for more. He couldn't resist imagining himself seated in her lap. The worn denim of her jeans looked invitingly soft, as did the excuse for a top underneath her gaping patchwork jacket. The pink gauzy scrap looked like underwear. His grin was positively wolfish as he announced himself.

"Daddy's home."

The dangerous purr startled Tessa. She cried out, pricking her finger as she lost her stitching rhythm.

"Oh, Daddy," Natalie huffed. "Look what you made her do."

He shoved the door closed with feigned ignorance. "I didn't do anything."

His young daughter's eyes burned with accusation. "You scared us."

He strode to the closet to hang up his jacket, struggling to keep his cool. "What is going on here? Where is your grandma?"

Tessa licked her lips, hastening to ease the tension. "I offered to spell Millicent for a while, so she could rest."

The crease between Steven's brows deepened as he turned to face the three of them. "She should've called me. I left the number."

"We didn't need you, Daddy," Nicky said simply, his cherub face beaming. He leaned over and planted a wet kiss on Tessa's cheek.

Steven could feel himself quaking with anger. Why was she making herself so indispensable?

"The children were interested in sewing," Tessa explained in the gaping silence, "so I brought in some of the supplies I keep in the boot of my car."

"A boot is like a trunk, Daddy," Natalie explained, rising to her feet. "Not a regular boot you wear."

"Thank you for the information."

Steven advanced on Tessa, his blue eyes drilling her with diamond-cutter intensity.

She shivered, feeling hot and cold at the same time. Damn it, she cared for him more than ever now that she knew the circumstances of Renee's death. And he probably cared a whole lot less for her after her angry flare-up yesterday. But now was not the time or place to find out. In a mad scramble she rose to her knees and began picking up her spools, pin cushions, patterns and scissors, heaping leftover scraps of fabric into a pile for the dustbin.

Millicent strolled sleepily out of the bedroom, a soft chenille robe wrapped around her pencil-thin form. "Steven? I thought I heard your voice."

"Hello, Mother."

"I feel so refreshed, thanks to Tessa giving me a break."

"Glad to help," Tessa said. "It's time I was off, though." She slammed down the lid of her sewing chest, secured the lock and rose in a fluid motion.

The children darted to her for one last group hug. They reminded her of frisky puppies as they snuggled and kissed her face. "Goodbye, poppets. Remember, we'll always be friends." With that, she bent down, intent on picking up her case.

Steven was quicker to the draw, however, and swiftly grabbed the case's plastic handle himself. "Let me carry this down for you."

"Steve!" Barry, who had been watching with growing amusement from the sidelines, tapped his watch significantly. "Time is not on our side."

"Yes, Steven," Millicent chimed in. "Tend to your own affairs."

Steven paused, feeling again, as he had last night, that his mother was hiding something from him. What had she been up to now? What had they all been up to? Getting the answers from Tessa was by far the most enticing option. "Don't worry," he said breezily. "This won't take long." With a wave, he hustled Tessa out the door.

"Right." Barry looked around once the door closed on the couple. He could feel three sets of eyes trained on him. "So, what have you chaps been sewing up while your father's been away?"

Millicent's brows arched haughtily. "If you'll excuse me, I believe this chap will go dress."

Barry stared helplessly as she walked into the bedroom, hating for any female to be cross with him. Steven would have to fix this misunderstanding before he left.

Meanwhile, Natalie had dropped down to the floor before the pile of leftover fabric and was rummaging through the heap with her small hands. "We've been giving our dollies brand-new clothes, mister. You want to see?"

He ambled closer. "I suppose. And call me Barry."

She uncovered one Galaxy Ranger from beneath the fabric, then two more.

"These are your dollies?" Barry crouched beside her, his gaze keening with genuine interest. The children viewed these action figures in a completely different light, a unique and interesting light.

Natalie sighed heavily. "Of course they're dollies."

"Monsters," Nicky growled. "Rrr..."

Barry chuckled at the two of them.

"Tessa showed me how to do all of this," Natalie went on. "I'm going to grow up just like her." Her voice was so matter-of-fact that Barry couldn't help but believe it.

"They're unrecognizable," he decided with awe.

She tipped her pretty face sideways. "Is that good?"

"It just might be." He rubbed his chin thoughtfully, aware of Nicky's hand on his shoulder. "What say we put the figures to beddy-bye in your father's briefcase? Wouldn't that be a fun surprise for him later?"

Natalie's face dimpled. "Daddy's sure getting a lot of surprises in jolly old England, isn't he?"

"JUST GIVE ME MY STUFF and let me alone!"

Steven kept a firm hold on her sewing chest all the way down the corridor to the elevator. It wasn't as satisfying as holding on to her, but it was the only leverage he had. "Not until we talk, Tessa. Outside."

She stormed ahead. One car opened, nearly full of passengers. Grateful for the company, she plunged inside. He was right on her heels, breathless and determined. Neither one of them said a word, not even as they hit the lobby and marched outdoors. Tessa stopped near the entrance where she'd picked them up yesterday, covetously eyeing her supply case before proceeding down Old Park Lane.

He trailed her round the building, spying her Honda parked on a back street.

"You must have come early to find this spot. You must have been very anxious about something."

Tessa unlocked the trunk of her car, wrenched the case from his hands and tossed it inside. "Get a life of your own!"

He slammed the trunk back down with the heel of his hand, causing her to jump. "I happen to have a life of my own, lady! If only you'd stop to notice!"

"Oh, I've noticed what passes for a life. Floating along without getting really involved. Swinging wide when someone like me tries to get close."

"If it's so awful, why do you keep coming back for more?"

"Why, you beast!" She stepped in close to make the accusation, her pert nose twitching like a bunny's. He pulled her even closer, his mouth curved in triumph.

"I know what's going on here."

"What do you mean?"

As angry as she was, as hopeless as the entire situation seemed, she was curious to know just what he was referring to.

He stood still for a moment, considering his words carefully. "I know you didn't invite yourself into the Sanders clan," he said with strained patience. "I know my own mother reeled you in. But can't you accept that there's no place for you with us? Can't you try and do that?"

She reared defensively. "I got the message loud and clear yesterday."

"Then what the hell brought you back?"

She rolled her eyes to the cloudy skies. Oh, couldn't she make him look the bloody fool in short order by telling him that Natalie had lifted her pearls!

Temptation gnawed at her as she fidgeted beneath his smug look. He was so damn handsome, so insufferably sure of himself. Of course, that part was her own fault. She'd made her interest clear. It was logical of him to assume she'd come in pursuit. But that didn't change the fact that he'd jumped to a conclusion and was a hundred percent wrong!

She leaned against her car, taking a steadying breath. "Look, Steven. I came to see the children one last time, all right? I swear that I wasn't after you, or your money, or whatever it is you think makes you such a good catch."

The wind was downright chilly, something Steven noticed as he regarded her thoughtfully. It tossed her golden mane and ballooned her jacket, reminding him of the skimpy shirt underneath and how cold she must feel.

"What are you looking at?"

"I was just noticing that you didn't dress for some innocent social call."

Right again. So anxious for her necklace, she'd grabbed the first available clothes and dashed out the door that morning.

He stroked his jaw, thoroughly enjoying this line of questioning. "Isn't that some kind of lingerie under your jacket?"

"No! It's—it's a pajama top." With a dignified sniff, she cinched the belt around her jacket tighter.

His chuckle was deep and spine-tingling. "Ah, my mistake."

It was clearly her mistake. She should have been more careful. But at the time, all she could think of was her family and the upheaval that losing the necklace would cause.

"Just give it up for good, Steven. I am." Holding her keys in her hand, she turned toward the driver's door. He was quick to stop her, snagging her wrist in his large hand.

"You had a nerve, returning without checking first. What if I'd already told the kids they'd definitely never see you again? They wouldn't believe another word I said about you or anything else. They'd be on the lookout for you for months!''

Tessa bit her lower lip. Would it be so bad if she turned Natalie in? Natalie didn't know the gravity of her stunt, the worth of the necklace. She'd only been dreaming of dowries. Steven would understand. He would probably even accept that the women had scolded Natalie and let the matter be. But she'd promised not to tell, hadn't she?

The decision weighed heavily on her mind. She was accustomed to doing exactly as she pleased, standing up for herself without a second thought. That was something she liked very much about being single and childless.

But apparently even other people's children had the power to entrap. In the short time she'd known Natalie and Nicky, they'd come to mean a great deal to her. She'd discovered a wealth of patience in herself, a quality she'd always thought to have in short supply, and a new sense of responsibility. What kind of woman would she be if she didn't keep her word to a trusting child?

"Look, Steven, I'm sorry—"

"Well, that's something, anyway." He pushed up his sleeves as though preparing to go on to another task.

"Hold on a minute," she squealed with a poke to his chest. "I'm not apologizing for coming back. I'm apologizing for not being able to apologize for coming back. Understand?"

He curled his fingers around her wrist and removed her hand from his chest. "You can't even keep an apology simple, can you?"

"Bloody hell, believe what you want. And let go of me!"

He released his hold on her immediately. "I've only been trying to be perfectly honest with you from the start, Tessa. For your sake and mine."

She lifted her chin petulantly. "You're fooling yourself, you know. You're the one who's scared to death to take a chance again after what happened between you and your wife." She gasped as she heard her own words. "Oops, I didn't mean to say that."

The color drained from his face. "So my mother told you even that," he said in a fierce little whisper.

"Yes, in an effort to help."

"Of course. And you can see what a big help it was."

They stood together a moment in silence, each feeling a separate pain, then Tessa turned to leave.

As she climbed behind the wheel of her car, her fighting spirit was at an all-time low. With a roar of the engine and a squeal of the tires she was gone.

CHAPTER TEN

"STOP PUNISHING YOURSELF, Steven," Barry urged as he eased his shiny red Corvette away from the Hilton's entrance. "How were you to know that Natalie swiped Tessa's pearls and she'd only come round to collect them?"

Steven stared out the windshield as Barry swung on to Knightsbridge parallel to Hyde Park. The drive to Franklin Butler's Kensington home was bound to be a short one. He knew they really should be tossing around last-minute ideas to spring on Butler, but Tessa was all he saw when he closed his eyes, and all Barry wanted to discuss.

In the end, Natalie had confessed to the heist, meeting him at the suite door on the verge of tears. She had wrapped her skinny arms around him and begged him not to feel sad. He had comforted her, thinking what willpower it must have taken on Tessa's part to keep his daughter's secret. For someone who claimed to have little experience with children, she'd proven to be a quick student.

Steven barely blinked as Barry whizzed by a huge truck. "If nothing else, it clears up her determination to flee. There was nothing she could say today that would've satisfied me."

"Do you realize how much simpler life would have been if you'd given in to her advances in the first place?"

"I didn't want to hurt her."

"And today?"

"I didn't want to be hurt."

"And tomorrow?"

Steven smiled faintly, thinking how ignorant Barry was about his circumstances. Even if Steven had wanted to face Tessa again, he knew Renee would stand between them. Tessa had to be wondering about the exact circumstances of her death.

Of all the women he'd met since being widowed, Tessa was by far the sweetest. She was also the last one he'd expected to ferret out his weak spot, leaving him nowhere to hide.

THE PARTY WAS ALREADY in high gear when they arrived. Franklin Butler's well-kept street was thick with cars, and his two-story brick house was filled with the sounds of classical music and laughter. A houseman in a white jacket and dark trousers greeted them just inside the door and offered to take Steven's briefcase, which was currently in the hands of Barry. Barry declined.

"Why'd you insist we bring that along?" Steven said under his breath. "It's full of the same old ideas and we're too late for our meeting now."

"Leave it to the master." Barry gave the case a pat. "I'll just drop this in Franklin's study."

Steven watched Barry head down the hallway, then wandered over to a portrait of the Butler family. Franklin had a good-looking brood, a boy and three girls, posed around him and his wife in the painting.

They all appeared so happy together. A loving family with a mother's warm heart at the center of it all.

"Wipe that gloomy look from your face," Barry urged, back at his side. Steven wondered how long he'd been standing there, staring at the family portrait. Barry immediately guessed his thoughts and gave him an encouraging cuff on the shoulder. "Cheer up. You can contact Tessa later on."

"It's over."

"Well, you won't mind then if I ring her up once you're gone," he murmured, waving to some co-workers passing from the living room to the dining room. "As a matter of fact, I'll use your blunder over the necklace as an excuse." He snapped his fingers and grinned cunningly. "That's it—I'll say I'm acting on your behalf. I'll explain that Natalie confessed and you feel like a conclusion-jumping buffer about the whole thing, too embarrassed to even say goodbye. I'll suggest I take her out to dinner on your behalf to clear the air. She's bound to carry on about you," he surmised regretfully, "so I won't take her anyplace too spendy. I won't make any moves right away, either. A light kiss on the lips...a touch on her cheek."

"Sounds boring for an operator like you," Steven said tightly, taking a glass of champagne from a passing waiter.

Barry, too, reached for a glass off the silver tray. "All I want is the same treatment you got. Pushing forty as I am, I just may give in and start my own little brood."

Steven grimaced as he sipped his drink. "You're only trying to make me jealous."

"I'm sure marriage isn't a thrill a minute, but—"

"Barry Lambert!" Franklin bellowed, stepping between the men. "I won't have you dissuading Steven from marrying that pretty girl in the paper."

Barry grinned. "Hardly. In his own way Steven's convinced me I need someone just like her."

"Good, good." Franklin slapped his beefy hands on their backs.

The head of Butler Toys was dressed far more casually than they were, in dark green corduroy trousers and a striped shirt topped with a cardigan sweater. And his mood seemed as relaxed as his attire. Maybe he'd understand about Steven's creative block.

"Happy birthday, Franklin," Steven went on to say. "Sorry we couldn't make the preparty meeting. "I had to see to Tessa and Natalie." The seductress and the miniature jewel thief. He worked to keep his features placid to disguise his rocky state of mind.

"Completely understandable." Franklin looked around again. "So where is your fiancée? Freshening up?"

Steven was ready and waiting for the question. "Well, no sir. I didn't bring her. She was—"

"Exhausted from a sewing marathon with the children," Barry interjected. "It's amazing what a creative powerhouse Steven has in Tessa and the children. All of them are so artistic."

Steven scrutinized his pal. Amazing what a creative line of bull Barry was stringing.

The birthday boy rumbled with disappointment. "Such a pity. I wanted to meet that girl." He rubbed his hands together with fresh purpose. "Well, in any case, I'm ready to tend to a little business."

"But it's your party, Franklin," Steven quickly protested, in no hurry to face the disappointing truth. "Why not enjoy your guests and save our talk for later?"

"I think I'll enjoy things all the more once I find out what you've come up with. Barry's call really piqued my interest."

"You called here?" Steven turned to his friend with a blend of disbelief and panic. The feelings only deepened as Barry nervously tugged at his mustache.

"While you were showering. I wanted Franklin to know we'd be late—"

"And that you had an ingenious new angle," Franklin finished. "Come along, then."

His study was a blend of heavy mahogany and supple leather, with enough books lining the walls to start an independent library. Steven watched with growing dread as Barry moved to the desk to open his briefcase.

Franklin closed the door, sealing them off from the noisy household. The room was quiet but humming with anticipation. Steven felt entombed, trapped in his own failure. Barry couldn't have come up with a brilliant new idea while he'd showered, and now he was about to risk any chance they did have with this clumsy attempt. Steven braced himself for the worst.

Franklin, in the meantime, had rounded his massive desk and pushed aside his high-backed chair. He splayed his hands on the polished surface, primed for a peek inside the case. Steven cringed as the twin catches snapped in the silence. When Franklin didn't release the indignant bellow he'd expected, he moved in closer. To his amazement, Franklin had his hands on two Galaxy Rangers dressed in wedding attire.

"It's a simple concept, Franklin," Barry announced in a clear, confident voice. "Just take a look at the Rangers in something other than their space suits. You have the bride and groom." He removed another figure from the case. "This third one is wearing something more casual, brown vinyl cowboy gear."

"Complete with clipped fringe on the vest and pants." Franklin grew pensive for a moment. "Yes, I believe I see what you're driving at."

Steven felt numb. "You do?"

Franklin studied him curiously. "Correct me if I'm wrong, of course."

"By all means, run with it, sir," Barry urged him with a wink at Steven. "Nothing's cut in stone. We're still brainstorming."

"Very well." Franklin lowered his bulk into his roomy chair and examined the figures in the hand-stitched clothing, deep creases appearing in his forehead. "I see the retroactive concept vividly, of course. Exchanging the futuristic jumpsuits for the kind of clothing we wear."

"Yes! Like a RetroRanger," Steven blurted out.

Franklin's face glowed. "Inspired name."

Steven ran a hand through his clipped brown hair, only to realize he was shaking. Things were actually on the rebound. He'd been saved at the final hour, like a man who gives his parachute string one last tug, only to feel that jerk and lift as the parachute released above him.

"I must say, this is a fabulous surprise," Franklin went on, resting his arms on his desktop. "I couldn't put my feelings into words before, but I now see what was missing—a warmth to your characters. I know how well they've done in the States, but they didn't come alive for me, personally. Until now. Getting them out of the space suits and into more recognizable clothing makes all the difference.''

Like Franklin, Steven was good on the uptake when he had the right spark to fire him up. "I suppose the Rangers could go further back than today's world—perhaps visit different times in history. Their adventures could be written up in the same kind of booklets as they are now, and recorded on cassettes, only with a historical theme."

"Yes, why not?" Barry said, not to be forgotten.

Steven winked at his pal. "I really think this could work, Franklin, if you don't tamper with the Rangers I've already created. I want to keep their legends the same, their suits the same—the whole damn package intact.''

Franklin's chair creaked as he rocked a little. "And add RetroRangers to the group?"

"Yes." Steven began to pace as he considered production costs and distribution methods. "It's going to cost a bundle."

"Introduce them over here first and I'll carry most of the load," Franklin offered.

"If you launch my original Rangers ahead of time, while we put this together, then I'm ready to deal." Steven extended his hand over his open briefcase on the desk. Franklin rose to shake it.

Barry laughed with relief. "Why didn't we think of it sooner?''

"Yes, why the hell not?" Franklin rapped his knuckles on the desk. "And who came up with these inspired designs on such short notice? Is it who I think it is?''

Steven stared over Franklin's head and out to the lighted backyard. Only one person had the means, the opportunity and the know-how. "Tessa's responsible, of course."

"That's why we were late, sir," Barry went on, craftily playing his boss in a way that Steven wasn't close enough to do. "His entire family was helping him put it together."

Franklin beamed with approval. "I've done the very same thing on many occasions. Why not draw on those closest to you for inspiration? My wife is my right hand and my children are extensions of us both." His expression grew sober. "It takes a big man to know when he needs help. And a lovely lady to step in and provide it."

"Yes, don't they have a nice relationship in the works," Barry chimed in with a grin.

Franklin shook his head in wonder. "Just when I thought we'd hit a permanent impasse." He laid his hand on the telephone and stared up at Steven. "I insist you call her immediately. Get her over here." He rose from his chair. "I'm going to return to my party now, to open the rest of my gifts. Congratulations, fellows. And you can be sure there'll be something extra in all this for you, Barry."

Barry rocked on his heels, affecting just a dash of humility. "You know best, sir."

Once Franklin was gone, Steven whooped like a teenager. "Hot damn, we did it!"

"You're very welcome," Barry teased.

"I am very, very grateful for all you did, man. Even if I'd seen those Rangers dressed in those outfits, I never would've been flexible enough or insightful enough to appreciate their potential so quickly."

Barry grinned. "You would have, eventually. You were just too worked up at the time." He sauntered over to the liquor trolley and helped himself to some brandy in a crystal decanter.

Steven couldn't believe his nerve. "Don't you believe in asking?"

"One lesson Franklin has taught me well is to use all the resources at hand." He lifted his snifter as an example. "In Tessa's case, it immediately struck me that she must know the designing business inside out to land a job with DeWilde's. And anything she might create for the figures was bound to spark Franklin's imagination. The worst scenario I could see was Franklin requesting additional time to think things over. He's a genius with improvisation and would have followed through."

Steven sank into Franklin's chair and stared at the telephone. Barry leaned over the opposite side of the desk.

"Give in and call her."

"Yeah, yeah, I guess I will." He lifted the receiver and dialed her number. After listening to her recorded message, he hung up.

"I hope she doesn't have a hot date."

"I don't think so. She wants people to think we're really engaged, remember?"

Barry shrugged and straightened up.

"Well, guess that's it." Steven lolled his head against the chair back, closing his eyes. "Get that liar's mind of yours going for an explanation. Why don't I know where my own beloved fiancée is?"

Barry turned and snapped his fingers. "Hold on now, there might be another way of tracking her."

"How? Radar?"

"Sort of. How about questioning Millicent? She might know what Tessa's up to."

Steven brightened as he picked up the receiver again. "You may just be right. For once I hope my mother didn't mind her own business."

CHAPTER ELEVEN

"SUGGESTING THE SAVOY to Gabriel was such a splendid idea, Tessa. It's always been your favorite, hasn't it."

Tessa lowered her gold-stamped menu to smile across the table at her Uncle Jeffrey. "It is our place."

To the world at large, Jeffrey DeWilde was known to be the brains and energy behind the DeWilde corporation. At the age of fifty-six, the president of the retail empire was in his prime, renowned for his analytical intelligence and formidable business skills. None of that meant much to Tessa, however. What mattered most was that behind Jeffrey's aristocratic features and cool, courteous calm was her treasured, soft-hearted uncle. Who had brought her to this very restaurant as a child, who had sent her surprise packages all through boarding school, and who, along with his wife Grace, was always on the other end of the telephone if ever she had a problem. It had been years since they'd dined here together, and her memories of the occasions had grown fuzzy, but the warm feelings could never be lost. This place would always represent opulence to her, with its glittering chandeliers, heavily swagged drapes, and its fabulous view of the Thames.

"I hope this invitation won't jeopardize your shopgirl cover," Jeffrey said in a lower voice.

"Though I would like to see it end soon. I nearly had heart failure when I picked up the *Guardian* to find you'd given yourself away as first prize in our contest!"

Tessa realized there was a trace of censure in his tone. And she couldn't blame him. The store's impeccable image was on the line. "It's almost over," she assured him with confidence. "Two reporters visited me in the department on Friday for a closer look at my designs, and orders for the dress I modeled are flooding in. Fashion reviews are likely to appear in Tuesday's papers, proving my worth one way or the other."

Gabe and Lianne appeared at their table then, just in time to hear Tessa's last remark. They claimed the two empty seats at the square table, Lianne pausing to squeeze her father-in-law's shoulders. "Thanks for coming on such short notice," she said.

Jeffrey swiftly rose to pull out her chair. "You look well, Lianne. Very well."

Tessa enthusiastically agreed, her gaze lingering on Lianne's radiant complexion, a perfect complement to her melon-colored dress.

"Sorry we're late," Gabe said, whisking his napkin over his thigh. "We invite you both to dinner, then show up last."

"It's quite all right, son," Jeffrey reassured him, easing back into his place. "Tessa and I have just been catching up over a drink." He took another sip of his whiskey soda. "Discussing the end of this charade of hers."

Gabe picked up his menu and hungrily scanned the entrées. "Despite the contest's crazy twist, I think

Tessa will get the desired results. Her designs are knockouts.''

"We wouldn't want the public to suspect that the contest was fixed from the start, however," Jeffrey said.

Tessa knew full well that Gabe was keeping Jeffrey updated, so she was a little surprised by his cross-examination. "We wasted no time in awarding another wedding package to a second essayist with no connections to the store whatsoever. It made the papers today—not the front page again, of course, but it was in print."

"Yes, along with that small article on Steven Sanders and his family." Jeffrey's pointed look didn't waver from his niece. "How nice of him to cooperate to this extent. Are we managing to make it worth his while?"

Tessa's pulse skipped as she recalled her encounter with Steven on the street that afternoon. Heaven knows she'd tried!

Gabe unwittingly came to her rescue, regarding his father with a trace of impatience. "It's all taken care of, Dad. We've sent him a credit slip for a full wedding package. It's good for the next fifty years, at any DeWilde store."

Jeffrey's brows lifted slightly but he said nothing. He directed his next question to Tessa. "So Sanders has no complaints?"

She nervously fingered the edge of the tablecloth. "Complaints?"

"You know, about his position, our hospitality. Anything along those lines."

Tessa could feel a nervous giggle rising in her throat. "He would probably say that DeWilde's has been altogether too obliging."

A shrewd gleam lit Jeffrey's eyes for the briefest moment. "How long will he be here?"

Tessa smoothed her flowing hair and averted his gaze by studying some of the other diners. "He's leaving midweek, I believe. So it shouldn't be too awkward."

"Awkward for whom?" Gabe asked.

"Him! Me!" Tessa spouted with a lift of her chin. "Does it really matter?"

Jeffrey nodded firmly. "It does to me. You're upset and I want to know why."

"Everything is fine," Tessa said breathlessly, realizing that there was no going back. It was now obvious that Steven was more to her than a fiancé for appearance's sake only. "I thought there might be something real there, but it isn't going to happen." She tried to relax but found them still staring at her. "Before you know it, things will be back to normal. It'll be as if he never existed. I mean, how real can instant attraction be? Once two people get to know each other, the shine wears off. When a whole ocean is between us, things won't be as intense as when we're thrown together hour after hour, time after time—" Tessa clamped her mouth shut, suddenly recognizing all the lines. They were the same ones she'd been using on herself.

Their waiter came moments later to take their orders. Jeffrey and Tessa requested their traditional chicken. Gabe ordered seafood for himself and Lianne, and a bottle of champagne to be brought round immediately.

Tessa forced a grin, grateful for the diversion. "That sounds delicious. I haven't had the good stuff in ages."

"Move out of that glorified boarding house and I'll buy you a case."

"Gabe," Lianne cautioned. "I thought you agreed to cut those apron strings to Tessa. You're like a mother hen!"

Tessa sighed and folded her hands on the linen-covered table. "I may as well tell you, I have no intention of moving, even once I'm established in my field. And that place is my own personal flat, not just space in a boarding house."

Gabe tipped his head back in mock wonder. "Really? Do you know that when I called you this morning, Mrs. Mortimer answered your telephone!"

"She has a key."

"Yes," he said in hearty agreement. "And was damn proud of the fact."

"She has access to all three of her rentals, actually. She doesn't mean any harm, Gabe. The poor thing was used to having the whole place to herself before she had it converted."

"She isn't just drifting round the place like a wraith," Gabe argued. "She grilled me like a sorority mother to find out who I was and what I wanted. She even suggested you could use a rise!"

Tessa clucked with pleasure. "Why, the old dear."

An odd little smile lifted the corners of Gabe's mouth. "She mistook me for Steven Sanders at first."

"Oh?" Tessa's voice was a nervous peep as she sensed what was coming.

"She didn't even give me a chance to correct her before rattling on. Such dear wee ones I have, she said. And what a lovely little family we make. She went on to congratulate me for reducing you to a lovesick schoolgirl and for bringing such cheer to her rambling old house." Gabe wagged a finger at her. "Apparently you've gotten along quite famously with the Sanderses in front of her. You know, Tessa, just maybe your hot little temper is getting the best of you here. Maybe Steven Sanders is right for you, and you're letting your own steam cloud your vision."

Tessa sighed shakily as her emotional wounds opened like tiny rosebuds. "I've been really confused about the whole thing. But I don't need your interference. What I need most right now is space—to think, to reaffirm my goals."

Lianne couldn't resist a grin. "It hardly seems possible right now. Your flat sounds like Paddington Station."

Tessa gave the table a small pound. "But it's not! I have plenty of privacy and I know what I'm doing. I don't need any more advice!"

The foursome fell silent as their waiter arrived with their bucket of champagne. He uncorked the bottle as a busboy set out fluted glasses. Gabe declined his offer to pour. With a nod, the servers exited through the scattering of tables.

Jeffrey reached across the table to pat Tessa's hand. "Like it or not, we can't help but want to protect you. After all, you are still very young, and you're reckoning with some mighty forces here."

Tessa knew it wasn't like Jeffrey to pry into her personal life. She could think of only one reason why he was behaving this way. If Millicent knew the DeWildes and the Montiefioris, some of them were bound to know her, as well. "You've pieced things together, haven't you, Uncle? And you know what the mightiest force of all is, don't you?"

Jeffrey nodded. "That's why I've been putting you on the spot tonight, of course. I want you to think things through completely and exercise both caution and discretion with this staged romance of yours."

Gabe looked at them in confusion. "I've been keeping you up-to-date on everything, Dad. We've discussed it thoroughly."

Jeffrey smiled at his son. "But you only know so much." Gabe's jaw sagged. "We're talking about Millicent Sanders," Jeffrey clarified. "Where she fits in and what she's trying to do."

Tessa hated to give her self-appointed guardian more information but saw that she had no choice. "Gabe, Millicent recognized me from the start as a Montiefiori. She's very fond of Celeste and realized that the pearls and my birthmark were a clear link. With matchmaking in mind, she encouraged the children to enter the contest. Her ultimate goal was to give her son the chance to fall in love with me and prod him into marrying me for real."

Gabe and Lianne exchanged an astonished look.

"I knew she was clever," Gabe marveled, "but I never dreamed she was that good."

"She had very little at risk," Jeffrey pointed out. "If she lost the contest, no one would be the wiser as to her intentions. If she won, her son would be confronted with Tessa and forced to deal with her."

"But the poor children," Lianne murmured. "They were so anxious for a mother of their own— and one who was a princess, no less. They're the ones who will be truly let down."

Jeffrey shrugged. "Knowing Millicent, she won't admit defeat with only one failure. There are numerous eligible ladies back in the States. I doubt she'll waste much time before dreaming up another scheme to find a suitable mother for her grandchildren."

A lump formed in Tessa's throat as she thought of being replaced in the children's hearts by some stranger. How quickly they'd gotten to her with their adoring ways. At the least, they had shown her that she could deal with children.

Jeffrey went on to tell a story about Millicent singing torch songs at a bistro on the Riviera one holiday season. He was obviously enjoying the memory, so much so that he waved their waiter away twice as he elaborated on the smallest details, sending them into rollicking laughter.

Gabe slanted Tessa a look of relief at his father's genuine pleasure. Since his separation from her Aunt Grace last spring, Jeffrey had gone through some pretty dark days. Grace had been such a part of him, a creative whirlwind who was the perfect complement to his practical, aloof nature. She had been executive vice president of the company and worked side by side with Jeffrey. When she left him—and the DeWilde corporation—to move to San Francisco and start a store of her own, Jeffrey had felt betrayed. To see him enjoying himself like this had been a rare occasion these past months.

All too soon Jeffrey began to wind down, his laughter slowing to a chuckle. "Perhaps we should have invited Millicent to join us this evening—and Steven, as well."

"No, Uncle, I don't think so," Tessa said tightly.

"But, my dear, it would have given us all a chance to have a good laugh over the absurdity of Millicent's scheming and ease your tension."

As if it were that simple! "Steven doesn't know who I am," she confessed with great reluctance.

"Why ever not?" Jeffrey demanded.

"We've hardly exchanged confidences," she said defensively. "It didn't seem necessary to complicate matters any further."

"He has enough leverage already, has he?" Gabe surmised shrewdly.

"Gabe, finding the love of your life has made you a hopeless pain!" Tessa told him bluntly.

"Here, here," Jeffrey seconded.

Gabe's eyes twinkled with merriment. "All right. I'll let you off the hook this once, Tess, seeing that there are other things we could discuss."

"And champagne to drink," Tessa said with relief, holding her empty glass in the air. "I feel as if we're celebrating something here but have nothing to toast."

Gabe grinned broadly. "Just you wait."

Lianne looked across the table in loving disgust. "Gabriel, tell them the news before I burst. Besides, the champagne's going to be flat if we leave it much longer."

"All right." Gabe removed the green bottle from its bucket and began filling glasses. The act of bypassing his wife's glass made it easy for the others to second-guess his secret by a heartbeat. "Father, Tess, it's my greatest pleasure to announce that my lovely wife is pregnant."

With sounds of joy they raised their glasses to the mother-to-be in a toast. Lianne lifted her water glass to salute them in return. "Thank you all."

Tessa leaned over to hug Lianne. "Congratulations. I did wonder if something wasn't up."

Gabe reared in mock affront. "You did not. This is our surprise."

"There were some small hints that made me wonder." Tessa sipped her champagne, wrinkling her nose as the bubbles tickled it.

"We haven't changed!" the couple chorused.

"Oh, no?" Tessa teased between sips. "It wasn't like you, Gabe, to be so dewy-eyed over the children's essay, and you, Lianne, have had a glow for days. All I can say is, don't apply to Pinkerton's for work."

Tessa glanced over at her uncle. He was almost glowing himself, and more animated than she had ever seen him. "My first grandchild. How we've anticipated the beginning of a new generation of De-Wildes. How Grace and I—" He broke off with a gruff sound and drained his champagne in one gulp, then stared down bleakly at his glass.

"How happy Grace will be," Tessa declared, deliberately trying to smooth over the uncomfortable moment.

"Yes," Lianne swiftly agreed, her eyes full of concern as she watched her husband's smile fade. "We have so many people to call—both friends and family."

Jeffrey looked up then, his voice and expression tight as he battled his emotions. "You must let your mother know right away, Gabe."

"I'd intended to call Megan in Paris next," Gabe admitted a bit defensively.

"You know Megan would impulsively call Kate. And Kate, being right there in the city with Grace, would immediately contact her." Jeffrey paused, studying his son. "But you know that, don't you. It's what you hoped would happen."

Gabe steepled his fingers beneath his chin. His voice was quiet and husky when he spoke. "I do talk to Mother on occasion, but it's still difficult to accept that she's set herself apart."

"She's still your mother."

And still Jeffrey's wife. The unspoken sentiment hung over the table as though Jeffrey had shouted it at the top of his lungs. Shouting would have been beneath him, though, even in private, Gabe knew. But over the past year, since Grace had walked out on her marriage, Gabe had managed to track his father's emotions beneath his dignified shell. He'd sensed the resentment and bitterness Jeffrey tried so hard to repress.

But recently, Gabe had detected a new, calmer kind of grief, as though his father had gone past anger and was stepping back to look at his life as objectively as he could. Gabe was certain that Jeffrey was tiring of the marital war and wanted his wife back. Whether he was ready to face this or not was another matter entirely. "Nobody's giving up on Mother," Gabe finally said.

"I have a good idea," Lianne said. "Why don't we all go back to our flat after dinner? We'll make a conference call to Grace so we can all share in the joy."

"What a perfect idea." Gabe turned to Tessa, who was seated on his right. "Will you come?"

"I wouldn't miss it for the world," Tessa assured him. She wasn't going to let her disastrous parting from Steven spoil her pleasure at her cousin's good news.

"Then it's settled," Lianne said, sitting up straighter. "Now, where on earth is that food? I'm hungry enough to eat for all of you!"

Their entrées arrived shortly. Tessa was just picking up her knife and fork when she heard herself being paged—with her phony last name.

"A phone call for you?" Gabe refilled their champagne glasses with a frown. "Who even knows you're here, Tess?"

"I can't imagine. Please excuse me." She stood up, smoothed her white wool dress and wended her way to the entrance of the restaurant. She identified herself to the maître d' and he directed her to the telephones in the hotel's writing room. She sat down in one of the comfortable chairs arranged beside an antique table and pushed the blinking button. "Hello?"

"Tessa?"

"Steven?" She didn't even try to disguise her shock.

"Sorry to bother you."

"Since when?"

"If it weren't important—"

"How did you find me?" She dealt out the words as crisply as a new deck of cards.

"Well, the children remembered you said you were going there for dinner."

"They're all right, aren't they?" The small catch in her voice was obvious, but she couldn't help it.

"Yes." Pleasure over her concern was evident in his tone. "They're fine. Everyone's fine."

She crossed her legs, then uncrossed them. "What is this about, then?"

His voice fell again at her terse response. "I guess I deserve this icy response."

"You did make it more than clear that I'm nothing but a pest—too young, too impulsive."

"I was hoping we could put all that aside for now—"

Tessa turned away from the only other couple in the room and spoke in a rough whisper. "In your dreams."

"You have every right to feel this way. And I feel like a fool even calling."

Tessa hunched over the table for further privacy. "It's not much fun, feeling like a fool."

"All right! I know I may have overreacted earlier."

She gasped in affront. "May have?"

"Okay, okay, I did overreact and I'm sorry. I also know about the necklace," he ventured apologetically. "Natalie confessed."

"Ah, so I'm all right again, am I? Natalie straightened you out and I'm not a desperate female anymore. Steven Sanders, you owed me the benefit of a doubt in the first place."

"Yes, I did. And I do appreciate the way you've handled my kids. They're so fond of you."

"Well, thank them. They're wonderful. Now, if you don't mind, I'd like to get back to my dinner."

"You must have a fairly affluent date to end up at such a nice place."

"The company's the best," she assured him with hearty honesty. Let him wonder who she was with—if he was at all interested. She'd done enough agonizing over his activities.

"And the food is great there," he said, obviously hoping to keep the conversation afloat.

"Yes, and my chicken is getting cold right now."

He sighed over the line. "Look, Tessa, I happen to be in a jam tonight. The president of the toy company I've been negotiating with would like to meet you."

Tessa gripped the receiver tightly, pretending it was his throat. He hadn't called because he wanted to make up. He hadn't even called just to apologize for jumping to conclusions this afternoon. The blighter was calling because he needed a business boost! She should have known it was something as selfish as that. "A smart guy like you must have been expecting a mishap or two along the way with this charade."

"I was, of course. And I thought I could explain your absence. But under the—"

"Simply tell him I have a headache. That excuse has been working on men for centuries. Good—" She lifted the receiver from her ear, ready to hang up, when she heard him shouting.

"But it's more complicated than that! Trust me, it is."

There was a clear thread of desperation in his voice, but Tessa steeled herself against it. Never in her entire life had she been rejected so thoroughly by anyone. His wanting her back as an ornamental fiancée was the final blow to her self-esteem. She forced an evenness into her tone. "You dissolved our partnership, so you can just live with the consequences."

"But he's counting on seeing you!"

"Then show him my cheesecake picture!" With that, she dropped the receiver in its cradle.

She returned to the table to find the trio waiting with bated breath for a report. "That was Steven Sanders."

Gabe couldn't resist pouncing protectively. "What did he want?"

Tessa affected a carefree expression. "Well, mainly he wanted us to know that the food here is excellent. Other than that, he really didn't have much to say."

Everyone at the table knew it was a bald-faced lie, but Tessa's snappy green eyes made it clear that going right along with it would be the simplest and safest route.

CHAPTER TWELVE

THE SUBJECT OF STEVEN SANDERS was long dismissed by the time they rendezvoused at Gabe and Lianne's flat for the conference call to Grace's San Francisco apartment. They'd hurried through their meal, opting for dessert at home.

"Good news can't wait," Lianne insisted. "Let's call from the study, so we can use the speaker phone."

The foursome crowded into Gabe's paneled retreat. Gabe set the telephone in the center of the desk and punched in the telephone number. Within seconds, there was a click on the line and Grace's greeting filled the room.

"Hello, Mother," Gabe responded.

"Gabriel! How lovely to hear from you."

Lianne slid her arm around her husband's waist and quickly summed up the situation for her mother-in-law. "Hello, Grace. I hope you're up to a family-style call."

"A Sunday night gathering?" Grace's voice leaped out of the speaker with vibrance, as though she were just in the other room. But there was a noticeable catch on the word *gathering*. "I'm glad you managed to reach me. I was just on my way out—"

"A luncheon date?" Jeffrey interrupted, glaring down at the telephone.

"Jeffrey! You're there, too?"

"Yes, I'm here." His voice held a blend of hurt and surprise. "There's nowhere else I'd rather be at the moment."

"You sound happy as a lark," Grace observed with unmistakable sarcasm.

An awkward moment followed. Jeffrey shoved his hands in his pockets and paced around. Gabe and Lianne stared at each other helplessly. Tessa quickly stepped in to bridge the gap. "Hello, Aunt Grace."

"Tessa! How are you! And how are those designs coming?"

"Wonderfully."

"The last time we spoke, you were still in Paris."

"Yes, Aunt Grace, that's right. A little over two months ago."

"You were in the midst of hatching a plot to deny your identity, weren't you?" Grace teased.

"There seems to be a lot of that going around," Jeffrey grumbled from several feet away.

"What was that?"

"Nothing, Mother," Gabe hastily inserted, frowning at his father. "Actually, Lianne and I are calling to see if you have any interest in designing baby clothes?"

"But I've only ever specialized in weddings!"

Gabe chuckled. "Who says you can't expand your interests?"

"Oh, Gabe, are you and Lianne expecting?"

"Yes!" the parents-to-be chorused.

"Congratulations, and thank you! I can't wait to be a grandmother."

Lianne tipped her head against Gabe's chest. "The doctor says I'm about six weeks along."

"We were just having dinner at the Savoy to cele-brate," Gabe said, cuddling his wife close. He seemed to hesitate a moment, then added, "We missed you, Mother."

There was a moment's silence before Grace said quietly, "I appreciate that, Gabe."

"We know it's late," Gabe went on. "Just wanted you to be part of the fun."

"Thank you, darling."

"It was my idea to call you first thing," Jeffrey in-terjected almost peevishly. "Nobody knew better than I how much . . . how much this would mean to you."

Grace made a wistful sound. "Yes, it almost makes up for their elopement!"

Jeffrey edged a hip onto the desk, as if settling himself in. "It more than cancels it out, Grace. They could have put this off for years!"

With an arm around his wife and one around Tessa, Gabe slowly and silently steered them out of the room.

Jeffrey, his back to the doorway, didn't even no-tice their departure. "Lianne looks wonderful. And Gabe's a sentimental mess. I should have known something was on when he chose a children's essay for the store giveaway. Oh, and you'll never guess who won the contest. Millicent Sanders! Not her person-ally, of course. She's trying to set Tessa up with her son."

"I don't recall ever meeting her son," Grace mused, as though searching her memory.

"I doubt we have. He seems to know nothing of any of us."

"Is he nice?"

"I don't know yet. But I will find out. So, Grace, did you say you were going out ... ?"

Gabe closed the door to his study and exhaled in relief. "That's done."

"And your parents are really talking," Tessa marveled.

"Dad misses her more and more."

Lianne gave Gabe a comforting pat on the chest. "There's nothing like a child to bring a family together."

Tessa couldn't help thinking how Natalie and Nicky had woven her life with Steven's in so many ways. Homing in on their needs had proved instinctive to her. Hearing his voice at the Savoy tonight had shaken her up. If the children had needed her, she'd have been at his side instantly.

Gabe reached over to ruffle Tessa's hair. "Sorry I dragged you back here, Tess. All Dad needed was a push in Mother's direction. He's already canceled us out for tonight, I'm sure."

"That's perfectly all right. There's nothing I wouldn't do for Uncle Jeffrey. And it's been fun sharing in such good news."

Lianne gestured toward the kitchen. "Would anyone like a dessert? Coffee?"

"Nothing for me." Tessa moved to the closet to retrieve her violet coat.

Gabe took the coat, holding it open as she eased her arms into the sleeves. "It sounds as if Mother and Dad knew Millicent Sanders rather well."

Tessa smoothed her collar. "Millicent's very proud of her connections over here. Now that we've revealed ourselves to one another, I imagine she'll have plenty of stories to tell us, similar to Uncle Jeffrey's one about the bistro.''

"She's quite a character,'' Lianne said, stifling a yawn.

"And quite fond of Grandmother Celeste. Do you know that Celeste actually allowed Millicent to wear the pearls on occasion?''

"They must have been close,'' Gabe said in surprise.

"The more I've gotten to know Millicent, the more I've understood her motives. The idea of matching Steven up with a Montiefiori must have meant a great deal to her.''

"About the pearls…'' Gabe frowned. "You didn't bring them along tonight as you promised, did you?''

Tessa opened her purse and extracted her car keys, not up to a lecture. "No, I'll bring them to work tomorrow. Straight to your office.''

Gabe trailed after her to the door. "Come early.''

"I will.''

"Maybe I'll walk you to your car,'' he suddenly decided.

"Maybe you won't.'' Standing on tiptoe, she kissed his cheek. "Sweet dreams, Daddy.''

THE LAST THING TESSA expected was company when she arrived back on White's Row. But as she pulled into the driveway, she couldn't help but notice the brilliant light pouring out of her bay. She emerged from her car, all the while keeping an eye on the window. It had to be Mrs. Mortimer, didn't it?

As if in reply, the landlady suddenly moved into view, her ample figure silhouetted against the glass. Tessa shook her head in wonder as she crossed the lawn. She'd mentioned Mrs. Mortimer's sentry role to Gabe in jest, and now here she was, waving to Tessa for all she was worth!

Tessa traipsed up the staircase, taking care not to disturb her second-floor neighbor Mr. Gentry. The retired postman nodded off shortly after ten and it was now eleven-thirty. She whisked open her own front door, primed with a pleasant-enough smile. Her landlady had made herself at home. She was seated on the sofa with a pot of tea on an end table and a teacup in her hand. "Mrs. Mortimer, what on earth are you doing up here?"

For the first time ever, Mrs. Mortimer favored Tessa with a look of consternation. "I'm taking you at your word that you regard me as a stand-in mother, my girl."

Tessa blinked in perplexity. "Well, yes—"

"Will you give me berth to speak my mind?"

"I suppose—"

"What on earth were you thinking, rattling your poor fiancé that way?" Mrs. Mortimer scolded in disbelief. "Why, he came over here and pounded the house down like a wild man."

Tessa looked around with a panicky eye. "I didn't know—"

"And our poor Mr. Gentry," she carried on, her plump face flushed in dismay. "Thinking the place was afire, he came scuttling downstairs in his socks and red satin boxers."

Tessa struggled to envision the wiry old man in that state. "Red satin boxers, you say?"

Mrs. Mortimer set her cup down with a thump. "That's beside the point, girl!"

Properly chastised, Tessa fell silent. She removed her coat, easing it onto a peg by the door. The last thing she expected or needed was another interested confidant. But she'd welcomed Mrs. Mortimer into her world as she would have her own mother, hadn't she? It was to be expected the older woman's intrusions wouldn't always be the most timely. "Well, Steven and I happen to be on the outs," she confessed, trying to economize her words and leave little room for discussion. "It's serious. My guess is our engagement will barely last through the fallout of the contest."

Mrs. Mortimer looked distressed. "Perhaps you shouldn't take such a hard line. He seemed ever so set on something."

"Not the right something," Tessa said firmly. "It's just gone all wrong, you see. I can't imagine he'll even come back here. I wouldn't count on ever seeing him again."

The woman's fleshy chin trembled. "Tessa!"

"I mean it. Do you see us together? Do you see him making any effort to mend our rift?" She folded her arms across her chest, thoroughly enjoying this chance to make him look the cad. "Well, do you?"

"You ain't seen nothin' yet."

Tessa cried out as Steven emerged from the darkened kitchen on the tail of his threat. Dressed in his dark suit slacks, a wrinkled white shirt and a loosened red tie, he appeared to have put in the roughest of days. The hard glitter in his eyes confirmed that he had.

She put a hand to her hammering heart as she absorbed the picture. "You scared me."

"You ain't seen nothin' yet," he repeated silkily.

Mrs. Mortimer rose from the sofa. "Now, dear, here is a man who's left his family behind just to settle your tiff before bedtime, so's you could sleep well. Is that the behavior of a cad?"

It was the behavior of a beast. He didn't want her to rest easily! As a matter of fact, with his clenched fists, he looked about ready to choke the life out of her altogether. But Tessa had built Steven up in Mrs. Mortimer's eyes and she was stuck with that sterling image. To the starry-eyed woman he was a romantic hero who loved Tiffany's and picnics in Central Park.

"Good night, Mrs. Mortimer," she said stiffly. "And thank you."

Mrs. Mortimer nodded her gray head and bustled toward the door. "Next time just ring my doorbell, Steven. Number one. There's no need to huff and puff and blow the place down."

The door closed with a thump and Tessa found herself alone with the big bad wolf.

She warded off a shiver as Steven closed the space between them. "I think you should leave."

Steven grasped her chin in his hand, forcing her eyes to his. "We had a bargain and you broke it."

"That's ridiculous!" She sniffed and blinked and tried to wrench away. It was no use. Steven had her trapped and wasn't about to let go. Why couldn't he show this kind of intensity apart from business? Why did he hide behind his career at every turn?

"We agreed to help each other out," he sputtered.

Tessa found herself weakening. He looked so harassed beneath his scowl. "So how did you manage without an ornament on your arm?"

"Ornament?" He repeated the word as though it were a curse. "As if you, Tessa, with all your drive and spunk, would ever settle for a tag like that! As if I'd ever ask any woman to."

Tessa's mouth sagged open. How was he managing to turn things around and throw himself in a good light? He was even making her question her anger. "So what was the emergency?" She listened to her own voice with surprise. It had come straight from the heart, bypassing her common sense.

"The doll clothes you made for the Galaxy Rangers fell into the hands of Franklin Butler tonight—"

"You're dealing with Butler Toys?" She raised her thin brows with a measure of respect. "That company's big over here. Tremendously big."

"Barry Lambert, the guy you met at the hotel today, works for Butler. Anyway, while we were down on the street, the kids showed him what you'd done. You see, Butler's been dragging his feet because he felt the Rangers lacked a certain warmth."

"And Barry saw something in the new image I gave them and made a presentation?" she surmised in disbelief.

"Exactly!"

She absorbed the new twist with a measure of pride. "It seems I just keep pulling you out of one mess, then another."

He bristled. "I see it as a balancing act, considering that you had such a heavy hand in instigating my troubles in the first place."

She slowly pivoted on her heels, running her hands down the sides of her dress, her complexion and eyes alive with color. "Some men find me rather exciting."

"All men find you rather exciting," he mimicked unhappily, thinking of Barry's interest. And Butler's. And all the anonymous hounds who'd seen her sexy photo in the paper!

Tessa's mouth twitched playfully. "Including you?"

"Naturally! Though I had other thoughts when you hung up on me without letting me explain everything."

"I couldn't have come even then," she admitted with traces of remorse. "I'd made a date and I had to keep it. I do have a life of my own, and I was up to my ears in it."

"Yeah, sure." His tone was one of defeat, but there was a real understanding threaded through it. An ambitious, vivacious woman like Tessa was bound to have a busy schedule. He and his family had taken up a great deal of her time during the past few days. And he had no leg to stand on, since he wasn't even pretending to offer her a commitment.

"So what's the status of your deal now?" she asked. "What did you tell Butler?"

"Oh, that I couldn't reach you. He wasn't all that put out."

"Well, good."

Steven smiled mirthlessly. "He figured we all have a future ahead of us, so there's plenty of time to pool resources."

"Oh!" She cringed. "He would assume that, wouldn't he. Too bad."

His features darkened, as though she'd slapped him. "Is that all you can say? Too bad?"

"Well, Franklin Butler, like everyone else, will eventually learn of our supposed breakup. String him along until then."

He grasped her by the arms and searched her face. "You haven't even hit upon it yet, have you."

His intensity startled her. "What are you saying?"

"The gold mine at your fingertips, Tessa. This is your chance to drain me good for those design ideas."

"Oh, that," she said dismissively. Naturally she hadn't missed the obvious. If this deal went through, there would be a monetary return for all the creative minds involved. It was so clear that he cared for her on some level. Why couldn't he simply let go and give it all he had? "You have my permission to take those little designs and run with them," she said. "It was a fluke. And you men are the ones who saw something there."

He gave her a shake. "You're too good to be true and it's driving me nuts!"

"No man has ever said that to me before," she blurted out honestly.

"Maybe not in those exact words, but something damn near close, I bet."

She smiled thinly. "I suppose so. Maybe it's just the reluctant way you say it that gives the line a different twist."

"Oh, Tessa!" he growled impatiently. "Nothing I do is right. It makes me wonder why you were ever interested in me at all."

The reasons why Tessa cared swung into focus despite her anger. It was because he was so loving, and so giving, even after all he'd been through. He was devoted to his children and humored his irrepressible mother. She too wanted to be part of his inner circle and bask in the warmth he gave so freely. When Steven Sanders wanted something badly enough, he made sure he got it. Looking into his troubled eyes right now, she was convinced he did share all her yearnings. But getting him to express them was another matter.

Tessa sensed she was walking a tightrope between despair and hope. They couldn't move forward until he was willing to acknowledge his feelings. And there wasn't much left of their London stay. By the time he found the words on his own, he'd be in a plane, flying across the Atlantic. Or worse, damn it, maybe a good speech wouldn't strike him until he was in a nursing home fifty years from now! "You know what really frosts me, Steven," she began in a goading tone. "You could have telephoned me with this Butler thing. You didn't have to come over here."

"You hung up on me earlier."

"You could've tried again," she persisted with strained patience, "And led off about Butler. You know I'm too big a pushover to shut you out altogether." It was clear by the flatness in her voice that she wasn't proud of the fact.

"So you'd be willing to meet with him?" Steven questioned with boyish hope.

"Yes, I'll do it! Set something up and let me know when." She threw her hands in the air. "Okay, then? Satisfied? Was it better for you in person?"

Steven swore softly. "Okay, we both know I could have called. But I came because I can't stand to be away...."

Her heart hammered as his voice trailed off. "Why, Steven?"

"Because you drive me crazy," he admitted softly. "I can't stop thinking about you, wanting you, caring about you."

His admission sounded stilted, but it was fueled with a strong, rich passion that made Tessa's knees knock.

He squeezed her a little tighter, drawing her against his chest. "When you hung up on me, I felt an incredible sense of loss. It shook me to the core, Tessa. Suddenly, I knew I couldn't leave things that way."

"I know what you mean. And I'm so glad you've come." Her body tingled as he brushed against her, reaching round her to pull the bright drapes across the window.

"You are so beautiful, honey...." He cuddled her close, squeezing his arms around her, burying his face in her hair. "I want to hold you all the time," he confessed huskily. "I dream about you all the time."

Tessa wound her arms around his neck and stood on tiptoe to plant kisses along his throat. "Am I doing this in your fantasy? And this?"

He groaned as she moved her little finger inside the curve of his ear, then flicked her tongue along the same trail with a purring sound. "Dreams can come true, you see."

He measured her with a faint smile. "Please don't put that kind of pressure on this, Tessa. I'd hate to shatter your dreams."

"I'm not— You won't—" Tessa sighed. "Whatever's stopping you from letting go, Steven..." She grew unusually shy as she tried to find the right phrasing. "I'm not worried about how Renee died. Honestly."

His finger traced the slope of her soft brow, his eyes darkening. "You can't help wondering, though."

"Wonder and worry aren't the same at all."

Steven swallowed past the lump in his throat. "Please, let's not talk about this."

Her mouth curved gently. "See, darling, you can do the right thing."

He made a ragged sound as her hand touched the front of his pants and cupped the undeniable evidence of his arousal.

Tessa gripped his shoulders, melding her body to his as his mouth found hers. She could feel his hands at the hem of her short woolen dress, lifting it over her thighs. His touch on her stockinged legs sent a quiver clear through her. She kissed him all the harder, and he pushed her dress higher, cupping her bottom, pressing her groin to his.

"Mmm, that feels so good...."

Her murmur filled his mouth with her own unique sweetness. He couldn't wait to really see her, touch her, know her. Letting her hemline drop, he reached beneath her hair for her zipper. Ever so slowly he tugged it open, groaning as he realized she had very little lingerie underneath. Nothing but panty hose!

The white wool dress pooled around her black patent shoes. Steven caressed the expanse of her silken back, reveling in her soft curves. She was so small, so fragile in build to accommodate such a dynamic personality. But everything about Tessa was unexpected. It was like unwrapping a tiny surprise package, not sure what you could find inside.

Tessa began to undo his already loosened tie and unbutton his white shirt. Sliding her fingers into the waistband of his pants, she unbuckled his belt and undid his zipper, thrusting his pants aside with a flourish.

Steven smiled at her with raw hunger. "I'm not about to change my mind."

"No, you're not." She went on to strip him clean, right down to his socks.

Suddenly that was all they had between them, his argyles and her hose. Stepping on his toes, he pulled his feet free of his socks. She followed suit, pushing her panty hose over her hips and down to her ankles in a practiced shimmy. She took the time to step out of them with care, before straightening up again.

Steven was riveted by her every move and felt overcome by the urge to possess her. The breasts that he'd admired for so long were all his now. He cupped them in his large hands, running his thumbs over their rosy rigid points.

A wanton moan of pleasure slipped from Tessa's throat as she swayed against his strong torso. The muscles in his body were so taut that she could feel their vibration. She moved her fingers over his ribs, his navel, his hips, squeezing his swollen shaft and pressing it into her belly. His sounds of encouragement and pleasure at her touch only heightened her own arousal.

For the first time in her life she understood sexual power. The strength behind blind forceful mating. It made her quiver with mounting anticipation.

Waves of passion pulsated through them as they stood there, locked in an embrace. Every nerve ending she possessed was alive, grazed by his coarse body hair, brushed by his roughened fingertips.

"I've imagined this so many times," she said with sweet longing.

"And it's even better for real." Steven could hardly recognize his voice, or the fierce admission, as his own. But judging by her answering moan, it was exactly what she wanted to hear.

"So I'm different from . . . ?"

Different from Renee, he realized. With intense concentration he closed the door on the flashbacks threatening to leap out at him. He hadn't felt this strongly for a woman since his wife, and that was reason enough to keep this separate, special. "You're one of a kind, Tessa. This is our time, just for us." He pressed his hot mouth to the hollow of her throat, kissing her crescent-shaped birthmark.

Eyeing the massive old chintz-covered sofa as a landing spot, Steven scooped her up in his arms. Tessa fell back on the lumpy cushions, as content as though she'd just landed on a puffy cloud. Kneeling on the floor before her, Steven kissed a trail up her inner thigh, inhaling her scent with unadulterated pleasure. He slipped his fingers into the soft opening to find her moist, ready.

"I want you inside me."

A deep groan rose from his throat as he eased himself over her, penetrating her with a swift thrust. His body shook as he drove into her over and over again. She never did stop talking, encouraging him, enticing him. Her voice was like an aphrodisiac, urging him on.

Their climax was fierce. She clutched his shoulders, crying out as a spasm ripped through her. It was her high-pitched wail that tipped him over the edge right after with an explosive force.

They lay together while their breathing calmed, then curled up together on the sofa. Steven felt warm, snug and satisfied with Tessa cuddled against his chest.

"That was quite wonderful," she murmured, nipping at his nipple with her small white teeth.

"No more of that," he rasped, pushing her mouth away with a gentle finger. "I'm still coming down."

"Happy landings, then."

He buried his face in her hair, enjoying the quavery, floating descent.

"I could stay like this forever, Steven. I really think I could."

Her husky, candid admission made him tense up. One union and she was talking everlasting. Maybe it was a figure of speech. Maybe he'd said something about it in the heat of passion. He wouldn't be surprised if he had. All his emotions cried out that she was so right for him. Frantically he tried to replay their encounter in his head.

In any case, this was all his fault. She wasn't the type for a fling, and he wasn't husband material. He should never have come here.

Tessa had no problem picking up on his withdrawal. What a time for her to get chatty! He hadn't been ready to hear those words from her. He'd given all he could manage this round and she should have been happy with that. Blast her big mouth! She hadn't merely fallen off the tightrope between hope and despair, she'd taken a deliberate swan dive!

But Tessa knew there were things about herself she couldn't change. One of them was the habit of voicing her feelings, without long deliberation or fear of the consequences. Steven tiptoed on eggshells, and she . . . well made scrambled eggs!

Steven didn't stay much longer, begging off with the excuse that they both needed their sleep.

"Another day of work for both of us," Tessa agreed lightly. She opened the front door for him, clad only in a purple silk wrapper the shade of her all-weather coat. Steven kissed her temple. A lump formed in his throat as the familiar flashy violet took him back to the moment they'd met at his hotel door. An electrical charge had passed between them without a word having been spoken.

Tessa struggled to remain calm as he hovered over her, his gaze pensive. "What are you thinking, Steven?" she wondered softly.

"Purple's just your color, Tess. Impetuous and unforgettable." Brushing his fingertips to her cheek, he left.

Tessa slammed the door. If ever she'd heard a kiss-off, that was it!

LATER ON, STEVEN TOOK OUT his frustrations on his pillow, punching it over and over again in a futile attempt to find a comfortable position, turn off his churning thoughts and get some sleep. He finally laid himself out spread-eagle on the mattress, exhausted, as though he'd taken a knockout punch himself. Despite his straightforward game plan, he was now fretting over a second woman and measuring his own blame for her predicament. And he hadn't a clue how to fix it.

CHAPTER THIRTEEN

DETERMINED TO APPEASE Gabe by returning her pearl necklace for safekeeping, Tessa arrived at the store nearly an hour before the official opening time on Monday. She took the lift straight up to the sixth-floor offices, crossed the beige-and-moss-green lobby, and remembered to stop at the large reception desk as any employee would.

"Tessa Jones?" The receptionist, who was about her own age and appeared to take her job very seriously, opened her appointment book, apparently for the first time that morning.

Tessa unbuttoned her coat, taking care with the shoulder bag that held her precious pearls. "I'm here to see Gabriel DeWilde."

"Hang on." The young woman handed her a small memo slip. "This note was lodged in the book. It says you're to go on to Mr. Jeffrey DeWilde's office."

"Oh." Tessa shrugged. It made sense, Uncle Jeffrey having a substantial safe in his office.

The receptionist seemed a bit disappointed when Tessa didn't appear awestruck by the redirection. "Can you make it on your own?"

After last night, Tessa wondered. But the question was a simple one pertaining to navigation. "I'll manage," she said with a smile.

She marched on, reminding herself that she was going to take Steven's lead and dismiss their encounter as "one of those things." Still, she couldn't stop wondering how transparent she'd been last night. Had he realized how convinced she'd been that he would surrender under her spell in the afterglow and admit to loving her? Was it the memory of Renee that was holding him back? She must have been a very special woman. Even Millicent, her mother-in-law, had adored her. And that, presumably, was one of the most delicate relationships known to man! But Millicent was ready to move on. She saw potential in Tessa. Why couldn't her stubborn son do the same?

Tessa breezed into Jeffrey's private suite, nodding to his secretary Monica, who was watering a large plant near the window overlooking Bond Street. Monica had the inside track on most of the family's affairs and had known Tessa for years.

She straightened to greet Tessa. "Ah, if it isn't our undercover girl! Good, you're early." She tipped her head to Jeffrey's door. "They're all waiting for you. In there."

All? Tessa's heart skipped as she knocked once and entered her uncle's inner sanctum. It was an imposing room, heavy drapes, heavy furniture. And the men present didn't add any levity to their surroundings. Jeffrey was seated behind his desk, and Gabe was pacing around the room. There was a third man, seated in a visitor's chair. He wore a business suit but didn't strike Tessa as the office type. He had a rougher, darker look. His mouth was set in an unreadable line and his eyes roamed like a surveillance camera. When he turned to study Tess, she had the unsettling feeling that not a single detail would escape his intense appraisal.

"Sit down, Tessa." Jeffrey nodded at his niece and leaned forward to depress a button on his intercom. "Hold all my calls, Monica, until further notice."

Tessa sank down in a chair and took an unsteady breath. Something was up. The tension in the room crackled.

"Tessa dear, this is Nick Santos," Jeffrey introduced, gesturing to their guest. "He is a private investigator working for me. Nick, this is my niece Tessa Montiefiori."

Tessa reached over to shake his hand. Her heart was pounding. Was this about the contest?

"Did you bring the necklace?" Gabe asked, placing a hand on her shoulder.

She started in surprise. "Why, yes—"

Gabe reached for the handbag in her lap.

Tessa gasped indignantly. "What's your game?"

"It's all right, dear," Jeffrey consoled. "We just want to examine the choker."

Tessa watched as the men gathered around Jeffrey's desk, where Gabe had placed her blue jewelry box. She promptly joined them. "What's going on?"

Jeffrey smiled as he set a loupe in his eye. "I just want to check the diamond settings."

"Why?"

"To make sure they're genuine," Nick supplied.

"Of course they are!" Tessa flared, not intimidated by the stranger's almost threatening manner. "Why, to say they're not would be to accuse my Grandmother Celeste of cheating me. She wouldn't have substituted fakes."

"The diamonds are still real," Jeffrey said in relief.

Tessa scoffed. "Why, even Millicent recognized the necklace immediately."

Nick's gaze sharpened. "Who's this Millicent?"

"An old family acquaintance, actually," Jeffrey replied.

"Is she showing an unusual interest in your family jewelry?" Nick asked.

"She shows an unusual interest in everything!" Tessa protested defensively. "But she's harmless. Whatever concerns you have, they don't involve Millicent, I'm sure of it."

"Calm down, Tessa," Jeffrey said gently. "Nick happened to be in town, and when I mentioned the pearls, he decided to join us today for a look."

Tessa almost stomped her foot. "Will you please explain?"

Gabe appealed to his father. "Please tell her before she challenges Nick here to a duel on Millicent's behalf."

"Right." Jeffrey leaned forward, lacing his hands on his tidy desk. "Tessa, the family is involved in an ongoing investigation concerning the disappearance of several pieces of our collection."

Tessa was stunned. "Several pieces of the De-Wilde collection have gone missing?"

"Yes, after the Second World War," Jeffrey said, his tone cooling with the unpleasant subject. "An elderly jeweler who cleaned the collection back in those days made the discovery. He was trustworthy and agreed to keep the family secret. Copies were made, and life...went on, as it were. But it was a terrible blow to everyone. Especially since the Em-press Eugénie tiara, which of course you know we display here in the London store, was among the missing pieces."

Tessa was openly puzzled. "Why weren't the authorities contacted then?"

"Because it was thought to be an inside job," Gabe said grimly. "The pieces disappeared about the same time Great-Uncle Dirk did."

Tessa gasped. "I thought he died in the war!"

Jeffrey shook his head. "No, he disappeared sometime in 1948. Dirk apparently tired of the family business and decided to start out fresh on his own. No one knows for certain."

"But how could he have gotten away in the first place?"

"Europe was in chaos after the war," Jeffrey explained. "All countries were missing records. Many people had falsified records to escape the Nazis. Authorities were often forced to take a person's citizenship at his word. It was the ideal chance for a man to start over with a fresh passport."

Tessa shook her head in wonder. "Being a product of the computer age, I find that incredible. Imagine, vanishing without a trace."

"The family set Pinkerton's on his trail in 1949 after they received a letter from Uncle Dirk posted in Hong Kong, but they came up empty," Gabe added. "Uncle Dirk obviously didn't want to be found. So much time has passed since then. Surely he must be dead by now."

"We don't as yet know for certain that Dirk is the culprit," Jeffrey felt it only fair to add. "He may have simply wanted a fresh start."

"But he was one of the few family members to have access to all the stolen pieces," Gabe pointed out.

Jeffrey flattened his hands on his desk, his features grave. "As for Nick's part, I've engaged him to make inquiries on the family's behalf. You see, the real tiara suddenly surfaced again. We secured it and returned it to the display case downstairs. And just recently the DeWilde Heart—an emerald, diamond and pink pearl bracelet—turned up in Australia. It's given us fresh hope that the other pieces are still intact and out there somewhere."

Tessa considered all that had been said. "But my pearls really aren't part of the collection."

Jeffrey's hazel eyes gleamed. "True. This check was just a precaution for your sake. The necklace has been many places over the years, and I wondered."

Nick stood up. "If there's nothing else, I have those other matters to tend to."

Jeffrey showed him to the door. "Yes, thanks, Nick."

Tessa prepared to leave, as well. "What a way to start off the week!"

Jeffrey tweaked her chin as she passed him at the door. "I'll keep the pearls here in the office safe, then."

"Yes, fine." Tessa slowly shook her head. "This is all such a shock."

"It's kind of pleasant to shock you for a change, rather than vice versa," he said dryly. "Though if you have any new information you'd like to share about that call you got at the Savoy last night, I'm braced for it."

Tessa laughed. Making certain no one was in sight, she kissed him on the cheek. "Steven needed my help in a business matter, and I feel I owe it to him."

"What have you to do with that man's affairs?"

"Nothing much. Later, then." With a hurried wave she was off.

Jeffrey shook his head, nostalgic for the days when Tessa and his own daughters confided in him at every turn. He felt frustratingly out of touch with Tessa's involvement with the Sanderses. And there was only one way he was going to get any satisfaction. By talking to the head of the clan.

"THIS STROLL UP Broad Walk was such a nice idea, Jeffrey." Millicent tightened the silk scarf tied around her chin and beamed at the striking man in the gray woolen topcoat beside her.

"Hyde Park seemed most convenient for some fresh air, with your hotel just across Park Lane," Jeffrey said, linking arms with her. "And it's a nice break from stuffy lunches."

Being fifteen years his senior didn't stop Millicent from donning a flirty smile. "You look very well."

"Thanks."

"I hope you don't mind that I brought along the grandchildren. They needed a good airing-out, to be perfectly honest. They're not accustomed to being cooped up at home."

Jeffrey smiled at the ragtag pair circling a huge cedar tree up ahead. "Actually, I've been anxious to meet them. By all accounts from Tessa and the media, they sound irresistible. It's amazing how they entered our contest and mistook my niece for the prize."

Millicent had the grace to look a little remorseful over the part she'd played with the essay. "They want a new mother more than anything else in the world. And Steven's been too wrapped up in his business to do any real shopping himself."

"You sound as though you're choosing his socks!"

"I wouldn't dare choose those!" Millicent scoffed. "He likes argyles as a rule, in a certain color and design. He has a special shop on Fifth Avenue where he buys them." She raised a black-gloved finger in the air with a triumphant sound. "Ah, but a bride is an entirely different story. I know exactly what to look for in a bride!"

Jeffrey laughed. "Oh, Millicent, you are still delightful."

Millicent's gray eyes twinkled. "Thank you, kind sir."

They strolled along for a quiet moment. The weather was on the warmish side for February, the sun having burned off the morning mist. They had a lot of tourists for company, snapping photos and pointing out sights.

"So how is Grace?" Millicent asked offhandedly.

Jeffrey cleared his throat and stared off into the bright blue sky. "We've been separated for almost a year."

"No!"

"I'm afraid so, Millicent."

"It's temporary, though, isn't it? I can't imagine you without Grace," she added bluntly.

Inwardly Jeffrey fumed a little, having forgotten how direct Millicent could be. "I'm managing all right, if that's what you mean."

She made a tsking sound. "Not as well, I'm sure."

"No, not as well. And as it happens, I do miss her very, very much!" Jeffrey was appalled he'd blurted out that truth to anyone, especially an acquaintance. But it was his voice ringing loud and clear in the crisp air.

Millicent pushed some stray silver hairs under her scarf, a crafty look in her eye. "Now, didn't that feel better? Telling us the truth that way?"

"Us?" he repeated bemusedly.

"Well, from your surprised expression I'm assuming it was a self-revelation above all else."

"Perhaps, Millicent," he agreed on a dry chuckle. "Perhaps."

She called to the children to slow down as they drifted farther off the walk. "I visit your mother on occasion, you know."

"Really?" Jeffrey smiled as he thought of Mary, in her eighties, dividing her time between her London flat and Park Avenue apartment. "She hasn't changed much in the past decade, has she? She still smokes like a chimney from that jeweled cigarette holder."

"No, she hasn't." Millicent smiled coyly. "And speaking of jewels, Jeffrey, did Tessa mention that we ended up with Celeste's pearl choker Saturday night?"

Jeffrey's mouth twitched smugly. One good thing about Millicent being a busybody was that she worked around to all subjects on her own. "No, she didn't."

Millicent's laughter was lighthearted as she related the dowry story.

Jeffrey chuckled over the predicament, but his eyes held concern. "Tessa's been under a lot of stress lately, and it shows. But I'm wondering if your Steven is the one for her. She's seemed rather upset with him all around, even though she'll leap to defend him, too. I just don't know what to make of it."

"And you've come to the source for answers," Millicent said matter-of-factly.

"I didn't mean to be so obvious. I also wanted to check up on you and make sure you're well."

Millicent smirked, dropping her voice a notch to a conspiratorial level. "They were mighty friendly as of last night."

Jeffrey's forehead furrowed. "But they argued by telephone. I was there!"

"So she was dining with you at the Savoy, was she? I knew she was going to be there. I didn't know with whom, however."

He was tapping the right source all right! Millicent was at the command post, transmitters tuned to all the right channels. "I was with Tessa later on, too, though," he challenged. "Up to a point..." He'd bantered with Grace for about thirty minutes at Gabe's place, only to find when he'd finished that Tessa had left for home.

Millicent's thin brows met over her nose as she prepared to defend the reliability of her information. "This was later. Much later."

"Surely you weren't that close a shadow."

She ignored his mild sarcasm. "I didn't have to be."

"So what gives you the idea—"

"It all falls back on those argyles again," she broke in, anxious to impress. "I was there when Steven kicked off his shoes in the middle of the night and I can confidently say that those socks were inside-out!

And as caretaker of his wardrobe, I can tell you they didn't come from the dresser drawer in that condition."

He pretended to shudder. "You'd be a dangerous foe, Millicent."

"And a most valuable ally."

"Please don't get your hopes too high," he couldn't help saying. And don't push too hard, he couldn't help praying.

"There are so many strings binding them together," she persisted. "Why, do you know that this fellow Steven is trying to do business with is interested in some doll clothing that Tessa made for the children? The man is dying to meet her in person."

Jeffrey's gaze sharpened. So that was the glitch that Tessa was talking about earlier in his office. "This English businessman is interested in Tessa Jones's skills, correct?"

"Yes, I suppose."

"I wonder if Tessa realizes how foolish Steven will seem when her real identity comes out?"

Millicent stopped in her tracks. "What do you mean?"

"Well, it's my understanding that they originally planned to skim over this engagement without making introductions to anyone. And that seemed wise, considering how complicated lies can become."

"Oh, I see . . ." Millicent considered the ramifications. "The deeper Tessa's involvement, the better Steven's acquaintances will get to know her—as the shopgirl."

"Exactly! Won't he look like a fool when this toy manufacturer discovers that Steven didn't even know that his fiancée—whom he presumably chased to London—was a Montiefiori?"

"Apparently Franklin Butler was pressing for a visit to your store today to meet Tessa. Somebody had better tell Steven before he brings those two together."

"And that somebody should be my niece, Millicent. No matter where this romance is going, she owes your son the truth."

Millicent hailed the children, who were sitting on a nearby bench playing some kind of hand-clapping game. "Please let me be the one to speak to Tessa, Jeffrey."

He agreed without hesitation. "I think she's seen and heard enough of me over the past couple of days, anyway. I'm on my way back to the store right now. If you like, I'll drop you at the front door."

To MILLICENT'S CHAGRIN, it was the pesky, beak-nosed Shirley Briggs who intercepted her in the Experimental Boutique.

"Good afternoon, Mrs. Sanders," she greeted hesitantly, her gaze slanting to the children, who were wandering over to the pedestal where Tessa had stood last week. It was now holding a pair of mannequins, dressed in bride and groom formal wear.

"Hello, Ms. Briggs," Millicent said. "I am looking for Tessa."

Shirley frowned at the children. "She's at lunch, I'm afraid. Perhaps you'd like to come back—"

"With whom?" Millicent demanded. "With whom is she having lunch?"

Shirley was taken aback by Millicent's abrupt manner. "With Denise, another designer. Is there a problem, Mrs. Sanders? Your son was just here, too, looking for her.''

''Oh, dear.'' Millicent's chin trembled slightly. Was she too late? ''Where were they eating?''

''A small pub on King's Road.''

''Did you tell my son that?'' Millicent asked anxiously.

''Yes, I did. Though quite frankly it's against store policy to give out such personal information unless there's an emergency.''

Millicent didn't give a hoot about store policy. ''Do you have a telephone number for this pub?''

''Yes. The designers are always on call, in case an important customer shows up.''

''Call her there,'' she directed. ''I must speak to her immediately.''

Shirley inhaled sharply, obviously determined to involve herself. ''Perhaps you should confide in me first. I'll then decide—''

''No, thank you,'' Millicent said crisply.

Shirley's gaze strayed back to the mannequins. ''I do wish the children wouldn't touch things.''

Millicent gazed at the pair, who were chattering away to the inanimate bride and groom. ''You call the pub, and I'll speak to them. *Now,* Ms. Briggs,'' she commanded as the woman hesitated.

''Very well, ma'am.'' Shirley made a mumbling remark about what Jeffrey DeWilde would think of all this commotion. Millicent curled her fingers, wishing she could tell Shirley exactly what he'd think!

The children had heard Shirley's complaint and went quickly on the defensive. Millicent listened halfheartedly, making a lukewarm attempt to admonish them. She jumped a little moments later when she turned to find Shirley standing directly behind her.

"Tessa's on the line," she reported. "Have you spoken to—" Shirley nearly lost her balance as Millicent flew by her.

Shirley glared after the older woman. "Why, of all the nervy, barmy—"

"Don't you say anything mean about our grandma," Nicky warned in a squeak.

"And we just wanted to talk to those mannequins," Natalie told the clerk huffily with hands on hips. "We didn't hurt them at all. And they might be very lonely. You don't know!"

Millicent picked up the receiver lying on the countertop, grateful that the children were keeping Shirley out of earshot. "Tessa? Thank heavens I caught you!"

Tessa, who was standing in an alcove of the dark, trendy pub, could barely hear Millicent above the din. She plugged her free ear and slipped as far as she could into the cloakroom. "Millicent, I was on my way out. My friend Denise is already waiting outside—"

"So Steven's not there?"

"No. Why should he—"

"Listen, he's probably on his way over there right now with Franklin Butler."

Tessa bit her lip, remembering her promise for a short meeting. "Oh, I suppose I could spare them a few minutes, for tea or something."

"No, you mustn't!"

"But I said I would. Steven expects—"

"But there's something Steven doesn't expect, dear. I must to speak to you before you speak to him. I'll be waiting for you here at the store."

"But I—" Tessa turned as sunshine and cold air poured in through the open door of the pub. Sure enough, there was Steven with a larger, older man sporting a bushy gray mustache. With a furtive movement she hung up the telephone on the reservations desk and ducked all the way into the dim cloakroom. Steven summoned the hostess, who obligingly checked the reservations book. Finding Tessa's name, she led the men into the dining area. Tessa wasted no time easing out the entrance.

Steven would have missed Tessa completely if he hadn't turned to glance over at a dart game in progress. The bull's-eye made by one of the players was not nearly as remarkable as the splash of violet flying from the cloakroom and out the front door. His mouth went chalky and his body wooden. She couldn't have missed him. She had deliberately avoided him!

Steven clenched his fists at his sides. She'd had a valid excuse for hanging up at the Savoy. But this... there was no excuse for this. It had to be a payback for last night. The only revenge she could think of.

The corpulent form of Franklin Butler hovering at his side was a very solid reminder that he couldn't tear out in pursuit of her.

A well-schooled master at concealing his feelings, even Steven found it difficult to disguise the disappointment surging through him. He'd only felt this hurt and helpless once before in his life, upon the death of his wife. Despite all his good intentions to steer clear of heart-ripping relationships, he was smack dab in the middle of another one!

CHAPTER FOURTEEN

TESSA PACED THE FLOOR of one of the boutique's larger fitting rooms twenty minutes later, wringing her hands and giving Steven's agitated mother nervous glances. "All right, Millicent. Denise is watching the kids. We're out of sight. What's the problem?"

Millicent was obviously primed for action. She sat perched on the edge of the satin wingchair, her wire-rimmed glasses in place so she wouldn't miss a thing. "I was speaking to your Uncle Jeffrey earlier—"

"Oh, Lord!" Tessa wiped her damp palms on the pleated skirt of her bright red dress. "Haven't you done enough?"

"I had thought so," she smoothly returned. "But Jeffrey brought up an issue that has me right back in the ring for another match."

"What does my uncle have to do with avoiding Franklin Butler?"

"Nothing, directly. Thinking as a fellow business-man, he pointed out something that you and I missed."

Tessa's green eyes widened. "There's another angle to play?"

"Yes. Whether you marry Steven or not—"

Tessa flapped her arms. "Where have you been? That's not going to happen!"

"Stop balking," Millicent scoffed impatiently. "I know about last night. When clothes come home inside-out, a mother knows."

Tessa could only wonder what had been inside-out on Steven. But if it wasn't his heart, it wouldn't do her a shred of good.

"Anyway," Millicent went on, "Jeffrey pointed out that if Franklin gets to know you, he's going to realize that Steven truly believes you are a shopgirl. When the truth does come out about your real background, there will be no way he can convincingly claim that he knew all along that you were a Montiefiori."

"Yes," Tessa said slowly, "I suppose it will be difficult for him to back up and say he knew all the while, won't it?"

Millicent straightened in her chair. "It certainly will. If he is told immediately, he might have a chance of saving the day. He can claim he knew all along who you were but couldn't tell because you hoped to make it on your own. That kind of thing."

Tessa cringed. "I suppose every time they talk about me, Steven digs a deeper hole for himself. He's already puzzled by my lack of interest to cash in on this toy deal. He and Franklin might be talking along the same lines."

Millicent clucked disapprovingly. "Why didn't you tell him, Tessa? Even as late as last night?"

"Because he makes me so damn mad!" she blurted out. "Sorry, but it's true. He refuses to reveal himself, but I'm supposed to fall open like a book."

"No matter how angry you are, you don't want him to be embarrassed on your account, do you?"

Tessa exhaled, sagging a little. "No. This contest has opened up avenues of success for me. And to tell the truth, your family's involvement has gotten me far more attention than I would have had otherwise. I want Steven's deal to run a smooth course, really."

"So you agree that Steven should be updated before you meet with Franklin Butler?"

Tessa pressed her lips together, holding back her temper. How could such an evasive man be such a nuisance? "I'll do what I can, Millicent. I'll make sure this is all ironed out before you return to the States."

She then excused herself in a flurry. Millicent slowly rose to her feet, both confused and disappointed. Could there possibly be a reason for Steven to have taken off his argyles last night other than sex? What kind of birthday party did Franklin Butler have at his place, anyway? It was all becoming a bit much for her.

THE ONLY PRIVACY TESSA could count on in her flat was provided by the security chain on the door. Even Mrs. Mortimer couldn't master that. More than anything else, she needed time on her own tonight. It was about eight o'clock, and she was busily altering a bridesmaid's dress for a customer who had become pregnant since the original fitting. Generally such things were done by the alterations department, but it was a rush job for a friend of Lianne's, so she'd agreed. Lianne had declared her a generous angel, when in fact she was only a heartsick mess looking for a project to keep her fingers busy.

The telephone began to ring, something that Tessa had come to expect over the past few hours as she continued to dodge a very anxious Franklin Butler. Why didn't Steven call on his own? Were the men together? The idea that they might show up at her flat was a concern. She simply had to get to Steven alone! She had her answering machine set to catch the calls on the third ring, so she kept her attention focused on the magenta taffeta gown draped on her dressmaker's dummy.

"Tessa, are you there?" Tessa's seam ripper slipped a little in her shaky fingers as Steven's deep sexy voice filled the room. She frantically worked to disengage it from the slippery fabric. "You've obviously been hiding out all day long," he went on to accuse. "And I saw you at the pub. Giving us the slip was pretty low."

Tessa weaved through the workstation clutter to the kitchen and scooped up the receiver. "Hello, Steven. I'm here. Sorry."

"Sorry? Is this a new game? You've put me through hell today with your invisible act!"

"Slow down! Didn't your mother explain anything? At least that I wanted to see you alone?"

There was a pause on the line. "Mother's not even here. She decided to parade the children by some old cronies of hers. Besides, she complicates everything she touches. This is simple, Tessa. Franklin Butler wanted to make a courtesy call and you ran us around in circles."

"He's been calling here into the dinner hour—"

"Why didn't you just answer and get it over with?"

"Because of you. Because of what happened to-day."

"Because of last night, you mean," he argued darkly.

"No, Steven, no," she protested. "I was all set to wait in the pub for you, then Millicent called and told me to run."

"Do you know how ridiculous that sounds?"

"Do you know how ridiculous I feel," she shouted, "being pushed back and forth this way?" Her eyes narrowed as she glared at the receiver in her hand. "Do you realize that your situation has grown far more complicated than my measly little contest? That you're now on the debit side of this charade? You owe me now!"

He sighed heavily. "Maybe I should come over."

She nervously tapped her foot on the kitchen tiles, her gaze straying to the living room, to the chintz sofa on which they'd made passionate love less than twenty-four hours ago. She wasn't sure she could manage a platonic conversation here, maybe even seated on the same cushions.... "It could probably be settled easily enough on the telephone. I simply wanted to tell you—"

"Save it till I get there. I have things to say to you, too. Things I want to say face-to-face."

"Like what?" Her tone sounded mystified to the point of insult. But she couldn't help it. Steven was a master at keeping things sane, controlled. Why wasn't he grasping at this chance for a safe, distant, easy way out? "If it makes any difference, I've gotten over the idea that we could have a future. So just tell me here and now."

"I've been doing a lot of thinking about us, too. For starters, if I was clumsy last night, I'm sorry."

Tessa's hopes rose a little. She looked to the sofa with new fondness.

"I'd really like to come over."

"Well, all right."

"Don't leave that apartment, and don't let Mrs. Mortimer in. And whatever you do, don't give up on us having a future."

TESSA BEGAN TO TIDY UP the living room, moving her sewing chest and dressmaker's dummy behind the three-paneled screen near the bay window and set her dirty dishes in the sink. Maybe she was a fool to believe he was ready to give in, to open up. But what else could it be?

She paused before the framed mirror on the plaster wall, fluffing her hair. Did she have time to change out of her blue sweats? Here she was, an independent woman all her life, allowing a man to treat her like a puppet on a string. Could it be anything less than love?

It wasn't until she heard a knock and the jiggle of her security chain a short while later that Tessa remembered the door was still sealed up tight. She glided out of the bedroom in an oversize red sweater and tights and swiftly undid the locks. Steven was waiting on the small landing with a gigantic bouquet of roses and an easy smile. She melted from head to toe. To think she'd almost kept him away!

"Hi." She took the flowers in her arms, noting that he was still dressed in the same gray suit he'd been wearing at the pub. It had grown wrinkled along the way, just as he'd grown some whiskers on his angled jawline. Sexy and vulnerable came to her mind instantly. All in all, he had never looked better. "I'll just set these on the counter for now," she said appreciatively.

He watched her head for the kitchen in that fluid motion of hers. Hunger filled his eyes. It was impossible to imagine flying away from her now. Somehow she'd slipped into their lives in one graceful swoop, and it all seemed perfectly natural.

"I'm very anxious to explain myself, Steven." She moved back into the living room, her hands empty, but her smile was brimming full of affection.

He shifted awkwardly. "I'd like to go first."

"Oh." She couldn't disguise her delight. He wanted to speak up!

"You really shook me up last night."

"Ta."

Steven felt a fresh wave of affection for Tessa, standing there so pleased with herself in such a bewitching, feminine way. It made him want to please her himself in an urgent, masculine way. "I can't imagine losing you now—or ever."

"Oh, Steven!" She wrapped her arms around his neck, resting her head against his chest. His heartbeat was as wild as her own.

He grasped her upper arms and gently kissed her temples. "I think I have an offer you won't be able to refuse, darling."

She tipped her head back and met his gaze. "Well, fire away, then."

He took a deep breath. "Okay, I want you to join us in New York—be a part of our lives."

"Yes, and . . ."

"And be a part of the Sanders corporation, too, of course."

She blinked in confusion. "Exactly what are you saying?"

"I know you're too driven in your work to be a full-time nanny, but that could be part of the deal, couldn't it? You could be a best friend to the kids in person. The rest of the time, you'd be working at my side as an associate, creating more magic for the Galaxy Rangers."

Her arms slipped from his shoulders. "So that's the offer?"

"I know it's a lot to ask, but the career change would be challenging. And I'll make it worth your while."

"How?" she asked doubtfully.

"With a beefy salary—and all our support!" He sensed her withdrawal and gripped her elbows anxiously. "Isn't that enough to shake you loose from your life here?"

Her chin dropped to her chest. It wasn't even close. What an idiot she'd been to expect more! All of a sudden she wanted him to disappear—for good—so she could get off this emotional seesaw. If she could end things without a foolish display, at least she'd have a shred of pride left. "I'm afraid I have deeper ties here than you know," she informed him evenly, making eye to eye contact.

"Ones that would cause you to turn down this opportunity? I thought that's what you wanted most—an enriching career. We can have that together, along with a very satisfying relationship."

Tessa managed to wrench free of him. She immediately put up her hands for space. "I didn't think
you could hurt me further, but you've managed beyond belief!" So much for keeping her cool. She'd
lasted about five seconds.

"Tessa, I'm making some major leaps here, trying
to make this work for us."

"I can't believe you've turned this into a business
arrangement!"

"It's a great start."

She shook her head sadly. How could he cheat
them both this way, when it was so clear they were
made for each other? The terms "nanny" and "associate" didn't fit the bill at all. "I'm afraid it would
take something tremendous to pry me out of London, away from DeWilde's," she admitted. "You see,
what I wanted to tell you is that I'm part of the family. My true name is Tessa Montiefiori. Gabriel
DeWilde is my cousin, and Jeffrey is my uncle."

"That's what you and Millicent were plotting over
today? Why?"

"So you could behave as though you had known all
along once people find out. Especially Franklin Butler."

Steven rubbed his chin, allowing this news to sink
in. "No wonder Millicent was so set on us meeting in
the first place. She thinks the world of your family.
But why didn't she tell me right away?"

Tessa sighed. "I asked her not to. I'm trying to
make it on my own steam with this contest, and I've
been keeping the family connection a secret from
everybody. It's all about over now. I expect there'll be

reviews of my designs in the papers tomorrow, and I'll reveal myself then."

"That would be a lot to give up. The DeWilde empire," he said in a grand voice.

"It would be a lot to give up," she agreed. "For another job. But we're not talking about jobs, we're talking about people. About you and me and the kids, and your mother and your wife." Her words tumbled out hard and fast.

"My wife?" he repeated on a dangerous note.

"Renee!" she spouted angrily, realizing there was no turning back. "She's the biggest piece of our puzzle. She's the reason you can't move on. Yes, she died unexpectedly, and yes, she was adored by all, but to go on in limbo, shying away from a new commitment... It's a tragic waste! I imagine I'm nothing like her—"

"That's right. You aren't." Anguish flooded through him, making him feel weak and defeated. He'd been right about Tessa. She was clever enough to unearth every feeling he'd buried along with Renee, and as strong as he was in other ways, he simply couldn't handle it. He did the only thing he could manage—turn on his heel and go.

Energized with fury, Tessa grabbed his bouquet of flowers from the kitchen and raced to the bay window, cranking open one of the panes. One by one she tossed the flowers down to him on the walk. "Let me line your path with petals, so you won't have another uncomfortable moment at my expense."

As he moved out of range, she hurled the last of the bouquet, tissue and all, through the window. It hit him squarely on the back of the head, causing Steven to stop dead in his tracks.

"Oops." Tessa inhaled a panicky breath. "I didn't mean to do that!"

He continued on, never looking back.

TESSA ARRIVED AT WORK Tuesday morning well before opening with the altered bridesmaid's dress, sheathed in plastic, draped over her arm. She was startled when Shirley Briggs, dressed in one of her tight linen suits, hustled to meet her out on the floor.

"You're late!" the prissy manager chastised.

Tessa sized up Shirley with a sour look. She was well aware of the time. She'd dropped by Butler Toys to have a word with Franklin Butler. It was the toughest bargain she'd ever kept, but she played the excited fiancée, confiding that she was a Montiefiori undercover and that she was unsure how she would juggle her career choices after she married Steven. She'd even brainstormed on further ideas for the Galaxy Rangers over tea, preferring a professional rather than personal subject. Finally, her conscience was clear. She'd done all she could for Steven. They were both free and clear to move on. If only she wanted to....

"I don't care for your tartness, Miss Jones," Shirley snapped when Tessa didn't quiver under her glare. "Just because you're a hit with the critics doesn't mean—"

"I am?" Tessa hustled over to the counter, where two newspapers were stacked neatly beside the registers. "I haven't had a chance to see these yet."

Shirley edged in beside her and put her palm over the stack. "Well, don't get too wrapped up in your reviews just yet."

Tessa's eyes rounded like a startled doe's. "Why ever not?"

Shirley's mouth thinned. "Because Gabriel De-Wilde wants to see you immediately, and he sounded madder than hellfire."

Tessa matched Shirley's snide expression. "Maybe he's just excited for me."

"No, I got the idea that your job is in jeopardy."

Tessa gasped. "That's ridiculous!"

Shirley beamed triumphantly. "Somebody up-stairs—"

"A reporter."

"Somebody after your hide is more like it."

That damn Steven! Tessa thrust the altered dress into her superior's arms. "Take care of this, will you? Deliver it to Lianne DeWilde."

"But—"

"She's waiting for it," she explained. "I'm doing you a favor really, seeing that you grasp at every opportunity to suck up to the family!"

Shirley's beaky nose pecked the air. "You come straight back down here when you've finished, Miss Jones!"

"As you wish," Tessa replied sweetly, easing away with a slight bow.

Most of the elevators were empty at this hour, so Tessa had no trouble zooming upstairs without delay. Once on the corporate floor, she never stopped moving, veering past the security guard and breezing by the empty reception desk. She burst into Gabe's office as though on the tail of a cyclone. "Gabe, I—" Her words choked in her throat as she came face-to-face with her accuser.

It wasn't Steven at all. It was his daughter, Natalie, sitting on Gabe's leather sofa, her skinny legs stretched out on the cushions like toothpicks. She was all dressed up in a beautiful blue felt coat with a matching rimmed hat.

Tessa slowed down, taking shallow breaths. "Natalie. Poppet."

Natalie extended her arm and pointed an accusing finger at Tessa. "Fire her, Gabe. Fire her right now!" she squealed.

Gabe dropped to his knee beside Natalie and gently patted her knee. "There, there, dear. Tessa's finally come. Now, I want you to tell me exactly what she's done wrong."

Natalie's lips trembled. "She's not my friend anymore. Not ever, ever again!"

"Don't say that!" Tessa exclaimed in alarm. "We'll always be friends. I promised."

"I don't want her anymore, Gabe. She...she made my daddy cry!" With that wailing announcement, Natalie burst into tears herself.

Tessa was stunned. Steven, in tears? It just didn't follow. "Gabe, is she here all by herself?"

He nodded, dazed. "It seems she took a taxi. She sent the driver in to summon me."

Tessa gasped in alarm. "Oh, poppet, that was a risky thing to do!"

"Somebody had to do something," Natalie said between sniffles. "Grandma's so mad at Daddy, she's taking us home today. And Daddy's so mad at every-

body, he won't talk at all. And Nicky's just a baby."
Her whole body shuddered. "I always gotta...take
care of everybody."

"Oh, my poor child." Tessa sank down on the sofa
and scooped the little girl into her arms. Gabe pointed
to the telephone, signaling that he'd called the Sanderses.

Natalie rested her head on Tessa's shoulder, but she
was still angry. "You hurt my daddy. How could you
do that?"

"I'm sorry," Tessa murmured, stroking the mane
of hair fanning across the girl's back. "Sometimes
adults hurt each other. And sometimes, I'm afraid,
innocents like you get in the way."

The door burst open moments later and Steven
rushed in, his twill jacket thrown over a T-shirt and
sweatpants. "Natalie!"

"Oh, Daddy!" Natalie raced out of Tessa's arms
and charged into his.

Tessa smiled wanly, feeling an incredible sense of
loss.

Steven crouched down and squeezed his daughter
close. "Baby, baby, you shouldn't have come here."

Natalie tipped her forehead against his with a sniff.
"Grandma didn't mind."

Steven's brows drew together. "She was sleeping,
Natalie," he said sternly. "You didn't give her a
choice. And if I can track down the cab driver who let
you talk him into this..."

"I would've talked to you, but you were exercis-
ing."

"In the hotel gym, a call away."

Natalie stomped her foot. "You would've said no! And I had to fight! She made you cry. I hate her, Daddy."

"No, honey, no. You love Tessa, I know you do."

"I'm giving back the prize," Natalie vowed vehemently. "We'll look for a different princess mommy for Nicky."

Steven looked up and met Tessa's gaze straight on. There was raw pain in his vivid blue eyes, and the dull sheen of surrender. The emotional impact of his vulnerability nearly knocked her over. He had nothing to hide anymore, she was certain.

"Leave us alone, will you, Gabe?" she asked quietly. "Take Natalie with you."

Gabe looked surprised. "Yes, of course. We'll just wander into the lobby to check out the communal candy jar." He held out his hand to Natalie.

She looked at her father, who gave her a nod. "I'll only be a minute," Steven assured her.

Once they were alone, Steven slowly rose to his feet, as though he carried the weight of the world on his shoulders. Tessa wrapped her arms around her middle, wishing she had the nerve to race over and cuddle him the way Natalie had. "I'm so sorry this happened, Steven."

"I am, too," he said sadly. "I'd hoped to get the kids back to their normal routine, with happy memories of you."

Tessa made an exasperated sound. "Do your family a favor, Steven. Either hire a good nanny or marry a good wife. And get the job description straight in everyone's minds."

"That's what I set out to do, find a nanny." He moved around the room, rubbing the back of his neck. "But none of them measured up. Then you walked in the door and everything clicked." He smiled faintly, remembering.

"Too much clicked for that kind of job, I'm afraid," she retorted.

"Yeah. Our fight jolted some sense into me. Proposing half a relationship to a vital woman like you was an insult. The only excuse I have is that my heart's been closed up for quite a while. The offer seemed enormous until you put it into perspective. Then it seemed like nothing at all."

She swallowed hard. "Did Natalie really catch you crying?"

He stared down at the floor. "Yes. You were right about a lot of things, but it all hurt me badly."

"Sorry I hit you in the head," she said, half smiling at how absurd the statement would sound to anyone other than the two of them and Mrs. Mortimer's tenants, who had had their noses pressed to their windowpanes. "But not measuring up to Renee in the final showdown was a terrible blow."

"You've got that wrong, believe me!"

"Well, you married her, didn't you, and wouldn't marry me."

"It's all my problem," he confessed hoarsely.

She touched his chest lightly with her fingers. "Surely you don't believe that you're truly dangerous in bed, do you?"

He smiled wanly. "I'd like to think I am, in an exciting way. But no, that's not it at all. You know, when I agreed that she was different, it was really a tribute to you."

"You don't mean it! According to Millicent—"

"Millicent's not the best source for what went on under my roof. In my bedroom."

"I see." Tessa's eyes grew as she began to speculate. Where was this leading?

"To the whole world, that marriage of mine seemed perfect. And it was, initially. Renee had always been a little self-centered, a little lazy. But she could be very charming when she set her mind to it, and she played the perfect corporate wife in public."

"Did Renee really die of a heart attack in bed?"

Steven rolled his eyes. "Oh, yes."

"Having sex?"

"Yes." He inhaled with a shudder. "The thing is, Tessa, she wasn't having sex with me. I burst into my own bedroom to find her with another man."

"Oh, no!"

Grief darkened his blue eyes to black.

"She was still very much alive and very surprised to see me." He shuffled his feet. "What an idiot I was. I had no idea, you see, that things had hit rock bottom. I knew she was a little discontented with our arrangement. She thought I spent too much time at work and neglected her. But it was only until the company was on a solid footing again. She grew bored being at home with the children, and somehow, in her mind, it was all my fault."

"How could that be, Steven?" she wondered.

"Renee was always good at placing the blame on someone else. Even when I caught her cheating that last night, she went quickly on the offensive." His face was pinched in agony as he relived the moment. "She began railing at me for not fulfilling her. I tell you, I didn't want to hear it."

"What about the man?"

"He was some delivery kid from a store, barely eighteen. He was nothing in the scheme of things, or so she said. Apparently he was not the first, either. I barked at him once and he was racing down the stairs with his pants in his hands."

Tessa could barely breathe. "So how did she die, then?"

"Well, our physician thought that having sex with the teenager must have taxed her heart, and then when she became angry with me, the stress proved to be too great. She lunged across the bed to strike me and slumped into my arms. That was it. She was gone. I called the rescue squad and tried CPR, but nothing could be done."

"How difficult it must be to hear Millicent go on about her, nearly canonizing her!"

"Yes, I'm tempted to correct her sometimes. But no matter what problems Renee and I had, she was a good mother." He shook his head. "If only I could get over the guilt."

"Why would you blame yourself?"

He was startled, amazed that she didn't understand. "I can't help but think, what if I'd been an hour earlier, before the kid showed up? What if I'd been an hour later? The kid would've been gone, and she might have had time to rest. Don't you see, Tessa, either way she might have lived!"

"Or she might have died right there with the teenager," she suggested. "How would that have been? It would have ruined his life and been impossible to hide from your mother."

"I never looked at it that way."

"That's because you couldn't see past your guilty feelings. You know, I'd say fate was kind. If it hadn't happened that night, it might have happened another night soon after."

His features brightened a little. "Maybe you're right. And the children were with my mother—thankfully. That would have been a whole separate disaster, had they been witnesses."

Tessa sniffed, her eyes welling with fresh tears. "Oh, Steven, exactly what are you afraid of? Did you think I'd treat you that way?"

"No, Tessa, no." He cupped her face with shaky hands. "I just don't think I'm cut out for marriage. Making another person happy is such a huge responsibility."

"But that isn't a spouse's responsibility at all," she argued. "Being yourself, giving your best, that's all there is to it."

"I did all that last time."

"Then you did everything right, my darling. It's this romance business you're getting wrong!"

He laughed at her blunt assertion. "Oh, Tessa! I love you so much."

"And I love you."

He curled his hand into a fist. "I want to marry you so badly, but it scares the hell out of me."

"Wait until Gabe starts drilling you," Tessa teased. "That will be any suitor's biggest test."

"Then we'd better get him back in here right now, because the idea of other suitors is more than I can take. I'm the only husband for you!"

Her expression sobered. "Naturally there are no guarantees, Steven."

"In a way there are, with you," he insisted. "In the past few days you've had to contend with more than most women do in a lifetime. And still you want me." With a low growl of longing, he enveloped her in his arms and kissed her long and hard, lifting her feet off the ground. When he set her down, they were both crying openly. They didn't even hear the door open, didn't know they had company, until Natalie's little voice pierced the silence.

"She's done it again, Gabe! Just look at Daddy cry."

"These are happy tears," Steven rushed to assure her, swiping his face with the back of his hand.

"Happily-ever-after tears," Tessa chimed in.

The receptionist appeared in the doorway just as Natalie was wiggling in between Tessa and Steven for a group hug.

"Sorry to disturb you, Tessa, but Shirley Briggs has called up here several times, wondering if you've gotten the sack yet."

"Hasn't she seen your outstanding reviews?" Gabe asked in surprise.

"I haven't even seen them," Tessa realized.

Gabe quickly retrieved two clipped articles from his desk and held them under Tessa's nose.

She anxiously scanned the glowing reports. "It seems I've made the big time. On my own merit!"

"As if we'd sack you," Gabe muttered. "You could do cartwheels through the store dressed in a monkey suit and DeWilde's wouldn't let you go! Even if you weren't family, we wouldn't let you go."

"What's he talking about?" Natalie wondered, studying each adult in turn.

"I'll explain it all soon," Tessa promised, tapping the girl's nose. "Right now I think it's high time I speak to Shirley Briggs and give her the good news."

"Have a good time," Gabe called after them with a cheery wave.

SHIRLEY WAS STANDING at the Experimental Boutique's central counter, ringing up a purchase, when Tessa marched up with her newfound family. Shirley handed the customer her bag, then turned to the trio.

"Good morning," Shirley said to Steven. "I heard there was a difficulty, but I never dreamed it was with you."

"There's no trouble at all," Steven assured her. "Just a little gathering to celebrate Tessa's success."

"She's going to do cartwheels in a monkey suit," Natalie told her, obviously looking forward to it.

Shirley frowned at all three of them, trying to make sense of what was going on.

The conversation halted as Jeffrey DeWilde breezed into the department, his patrician features alight with pleasure. "Good morning, one and all!"

"Good morning!" Tessa and Shirley called out in unison.

"I wanted to come by and offer my congratulations personally, Tessa."

Tessa winked, stepping back to give Jeffrey a clear view of Natalie and Steven. "These are the Sanderses. I'd like you to meet Steven Sanders and his daughter Natalie."

Jeffrey extended his hand to Steven. "It's a pleasure to meet you. Though I feel I already know you through Millicent."

Tessa could see Shirley was mentally treading water, struggling to keep in the swim of things. She was probably musing over Jeffrey's connection to Millicent and reviewing how she'd treated the older woman.

"How thoughtful of you to come in this way, Mr. DeWilde," Shirley said, obviously eager to have him acknowledge her presence.

Jeffrey measured her through narrowed eyes.

"What do you think of Tessa here, garnering the spotlight with her designs?" he asked. "That contest certainly did the trick, didn't it?"

"She's done splendidly, sir." Shirley regarded Tessa with feigned approval. Tessa half hoped the woman would argue that the promotional scheme was her brainchild, but apparently she didn't have the nerve. "What will we do next?"

"A good question," Jeffrey heartily agreed. "You know, Miss Briggs, as happy as I am with the boutique, I'd like to see more input from family members. How would you take to sharing your authority with a DeWilde relative who really knows her stuff?"

Shirley considered the idea. "Is there a relative interested in me and my modest operation?"

"There is indeed," Jeffrey informed her with a sweeping gesture. "Allow me to introduce you to

Tessa Montiefiori. Shirley, my niece. She's been masquerading as a shopgirl to gain respect in her field. But now that she's proven herself, there's no reason for it any longer.''

Shirley pressed a hand to her bosom and her mouth sagged open. ''Why, it can't be! We could never collaborate.''

Jeffrey paused, as if to give the situation further thought. ''You're right. Perhaps it would be better if Tessa took on a senior position. I'll create one just above yours.''

Shirley was aghast. She leaned against the glass counter. ''I would be the laughingstock of the store!''

''There's nothing funny about the way you've systematically stolen ideas from your subordinates,'' Tessa scolded. ''And I have a right to complain—as one of your victims!''

Shirley's complexion turned fire engine red. ''I suppose no one would believe *my* side of the story.''

''You've stepped on too many toes to rally support,'' Tessa concurred.

''Well, then. It seems best if I clear out altogether.'' Shirley moved toward the fitting rooms, her nose in the air.

Tessa laughed. ''Good show, Uncle Jeffrey.''

Jeffrey's lips twitched, but he kept a passive expression. ''It wasn't until last night, when Gabe and I were reviewing this department's future, that he filled me in on Shirley's antics. How low of her to steal her employees' ideas. I simply won't stand for it. I still have no idea how we hired that woman, anyway.''

Tessa shook her finger at him. "That was quite a trap you set for her. Your pensive pauses seemed quite genuine."

"All for your amusement, my dear. A small reward for tolerating her." Jeffrey released a heartfelt sigh. "Now that this department is on the upswing, I suppose I'll be losing my best help."

"Not at all," Tessa objected.

Jeffrey frowned at Steven. "Are you letting this girl get away, Sanders?"

"No, sir," Steven blurted out in surprise. "It's my intention to pack her off to New York if she's willing."

"I mean that Denise is perfectly capable of taking the reins," Tessa hastened to clarify. "I will be joining Steven."

"Our New York branch will be pleased to have you, if that's what you want."

Natalie latched herself onto Tessa's arm with lightning speed. "She's going to be real busy. We'll let you know."

The adults broke into laughter.

EPILOGUE

"HURRY UP, GABE," Lianne called out, popping a tape into their video player. "The show must go on!"

Gabe rushed into the living room to meet not only his wife's impatient glance, but Jeffrey's and Mrs. Mortimer's, as well. "Sorry. I was stirring the stew Mrs. Mortimer brought along for our dinner. Go ahead and play the tape."

Lianne aimed the remote control at the television and pressed the start button. The screen came to life with Natalie's cheery little face.

"Hello everybody." The camera pulled back to reveal a lavish swimming pool in a climate boasting sunshine and palm trees, far, far away from chilly, foggy London. Natalie was wearing a yellow swimsuit and waving merrily.

"It's been three days since we left jolly old England," she chirped in greeting. "And I bet you want to know what we're doing. Well, we all got married in Las Vegas today. We eloped."

Murmurs of pleasure filled the room.

"Nicky wanted to go through a drive-in chapel, but Daddy said it was too rush-rush, and Mommy wanted to wear her wedding dress. We're going back to New York tomorrow. Nicky and I have school, and Tessa—I mean, Mommy—and Daddy have to work on the Rangers for Mr. Butler. Grandma Milly is staying here a few more days. She ran into some old friends at the casino and kissed a man who smokes cigars.

"Anyway, we'll be visiting all of you in the summertime."

Natalie looked at someone off camera and crooked her finger. "Come say goodbye, Nicky." Nicky came scampering into range dressed in a red swimsuit. He bypassed his sister and did a cannonball into the pool.

Natalie, dripping wet, stomped her foot in disgust. "Daddy, he's being a behavior problem again!"

Tessa moved into view, dressed in her bridal gown, with a towel for Natalie.

"Lovely, charming," Lianne and Mrs. Mortimer approved unanimously.

Tessa smiled. "I thought you'd like to see me wearing this for real, Gabe." She waved to the camera, then gingerly moved to the edge of the pool. She extended her hand to Nicky. "C'mon, Nicky. Careful, now."

To everyone's amazement, Nicky gave his new mother a hard tug, sending her reeling into the water with a scream.

Natalie clamped her hands to her miniscule hips. "My whole movie is ruined!"

The camera zoomed in on her. She turned and slid her finger across her throat. "Cut, Daddy, cut!" With that order she jumped into the pool herself.

"Cut," Steven said as the camera panned the three bobbing figures. "And print."

The screen went blank then. Groans and laughter rose from the audience.

The television screen went blank and everyone stood up, talking at once.

"I guess I'm finally off the hook," Gabe said. "Tessa's another man's responsibility now."

"I doubt that will stop you from interfering in her life," Lianne retorted, giving him a playful nudge.

"Tessa simply brings out the best in all of us," Mrs. Mortimer declared, her bosom lifting with a heartfelt sigh. "And I can't thank you enough for including me in this viewing. I've been so concerned, what with everything happening as fast as it did."

"Tessa mentioned you specifically in her note," Jeffrey said, offering the landlady his arm. "And I must say she has wonderful taste in friends. Shall we sample some of your stew? It smells marvelous."

"Let's do," Gabe agreed, taking Mrs. Mortimer's other arm. "I've been dying for some since the moment I first smelled it on the simmer. It was the day I came to your house to compliment Tessa on her choice of flats."

WEDDINGS BY DeWILDE

continues with

TO LOVE A THIEF

by Margaret St. George

Available in September

Here's a preview!

TO LOVE A THIEF

"HOW LONG HAVE you been watching my house, spying on me?" she whispered. His mouth was perfectly shaped for kissing, for murmuring words of love.

"Long enough that I know you jog for forty-five minutes every morning. When you return, you cool down beside that chestnut tree, then watch the sun on the sea while you drink a glass of orange juice." He tilted her face up to his and brushed his thumb across her mouth, then he kissed her.

Allison's eyes closed and she sagged against his body as if his kiss drained her of resistance and the energy to stand upright. "What else?" she whispered, her voice husky.

He kissed her deeply then, exploring the taste of her, the shape of her lips, the feel of her body pressed next to his. "You don't seem to have servants," he murmured. "But a man came to trim the gardens the day before yesterday. As the terraces are well maintained, I assume he comes once a week."

They kissed again, this time with growing heat and urgency. "He does," Allison conceded, her reply no louder than a moan.

Paul's hands slipped to her hips and he fitted her body against his, letting her feel the heat and hardness of his arousal. A tremor shot through her limbs.

"I've always heard that uniforms turn women on, but I didn't know it worked in reverse, she murmured. "Or do you get this passionate about all phone company employees?"

When Allison opened her eyes, she found him looking down at her. There was no mistaking the deepening desire that smoldered in his gaze. When she'd told him to open the toolbox and when he'd found Madame Trazakis's figurines within, they had entered a new phase. Paul trusted her now, and his trust allowed him to go forward personally as well as professionally. He had wanted her from the beginning, she knew that. Now he was free to pursue his desires.

But what about her?

A look of confusion clouded her eyes. "I don't know why I'm doing this," she said softly. "What is it about you that's made me throw aside good sense and everything I believe in?" Right now, with his arms around her and his lips nuzzling her throat, she doubted she could remember the principles she claimed to hold dear.

"Whatever it is," he said hoarsely, speaking against her breasts, "the same thing has happened to me."

HARLEQUIN®

Don't miss these Harlequin favorites by some of our most distinguished authors!
And now, you can receive a discount by ordering two or more titles!

HT #25663	THE LAWMAN by Vicki Lewis Thompson	$3.25 U.S.☐/$3.75 CAN. ☐
HP #11788	THE SISTER SWAP by Susan Napier	$3.25 U.S.☐/$3.75 CAN. ☐
HR #03293	THE MAN WHO CAME FOR CHRISTMAS by Bethany Campbell	$2.99 U.S.☐/$3.50 CAN. ☐
HS #70667	FATHERS & OTHER STRANGERS by Evelyn Crowe	$3.75 U.S.☐/$4.25 CAN. ☐
HI #22198	MURDER BY THE BOOK by Margaret St. George	$2.89 ☐
HAR #16520	THE ADVENTURESS by M.J. Rodgers	$3.50 U.S.☐/$3.99 CAN. ☐
HH #28885	DESERT ROGUE by Erin Yorke	$4.50 U.S.☐/$4.99 CAN. ☐

(limited quantities available on certain titles)

	AMOUNT	$
DEDUCT:	10% DISCOUNT FOR 2+ BOOKS	$
ADD:	POSTAGE & HANDLING	$
	($1.00 for one book, 50¢ for each additional)	
	APPLICABLE TAXES**	$_____
	TOTAL PAYABLE	$_____
	(check or money order—please do not send cash)	

To order, complete this form and send it, along with a check or money order for the total above, payable to Harlequin Books, to: **In the U.S.:** 3010 Walden Avenue, P.O. Box 9047, Buffalo, NY 14269-9047; **In Canada:** P.O. Box 613, Fort Erie, Ontario, L2A 5X3.

Name:_____

Address:_____ City:_____

State/Prov.:_____ Zip/Postal Code:_____

**New York residents remit applicable sales taxes.
Canadian residents remit applicable GST and provincial taxes.

HBACK-JS3

Look us up on-line at: http://www.romance.net

WAYS TO UNEXPECTEDLY MEET MR. RIGHT:

♡ *Go out with the sexy-sounding stranger
your daughter secretly set you up with
through a personal ad.*

♡ *RSVP yes to a wedding invitation—soon
it might be your turn to say "I do!"*

♡ *Receive a marriage proposal by mail—
from a man you've never met....*

*These are just a few of the unexpected
ways that written communication
leads to love in Silhouette Yours Truly.*

*Each month, look for two fast-paced, fun and
flirtatious Yours Truly novels
(with entertaining treats and sneak previews
in the back pages) by some of your favorite
authors—and some who are sure to
become favorites.*

YOURS TRULY™:
Love—when you least expect it!

HARLEQUIN PRESENTS®

HARLEQUIN PRESENTS
men you won't be able to resist falling in love with...

HARLEQUIN PRESENTS
women who have feelings just like your own...

HARLEQUIN PRESENTS
powerful passion in exotic international settings...

HARLEQUIN PRESENTS
intense, dramatic stories that will keep you turning
to the very last page...

HARLEQUIN PRESENTS
The world's bestselling romance series!

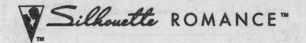

What's a single dad to do when he needs a wife by next Thursday?

Who's a confirmed bachelor to call when he finds a baby on his doorstep?

How does a plain Jane in love with her gorgeous boss get him to notice her?

From classic love stories to romantic comedies to emotional heart tuggers, **Silhouette Romance** offers six irresistible novels every month by some of your favorite authors!
Such as...beloved bestsellers **Diana Palmer,**
Annette Broadrick, Suzanne Carey, Elizabeth August
and **Marie Ferrarella,** to name just a few—and some sure to become favorites!

Fabulous Fathers...Bundles of Joy...Miniseries...
Months of blushing brides and convenient weddings...
Holiday celebrations... You'll find all this and much more in
Silhouette Romance—always emotional, always enjoyable, always about love!

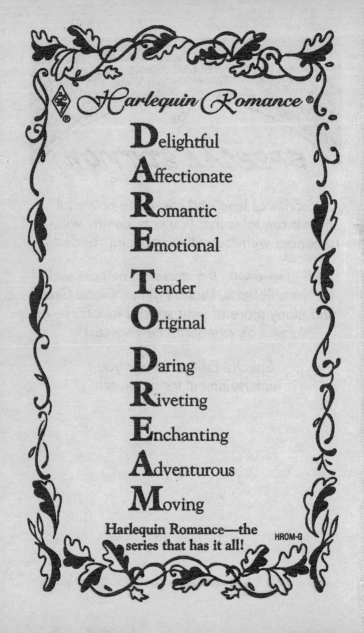

Harlequin Romance ®

Delightful

Affectionate

Romantic

Emotional

Tender

Original

Daring

Riveting

Enchanting

Adventurous

Moving

Harlequin Romance—the
series that has it all!

HROM-G